ACQUAINTED WITH VICE

A BODY POSITIVE MM AGE GAP ROMANCE

SIOBHAN SMILE

HOSTILE WHISPERS PRESS

Acquainted with *Vice*

Siobhan Smile

Hostile
WHISPERS PRESS

For my readers who believe like me that everyone is worthy of love, respect and a happily ever after.

ACQUAINTED WITH VICE
A BODY POSITIVE MM AGE GAP ROMANCE

Lee

Starting over after fifteen years hadn't crossed my mind, but the reality hit me when the final divorce papers arrived. To process the end of my marriage, I'd escaped to the lake where I owned a home. I was determined to have everything figured out by the time I returned to the city. What happened instead was an ambush by my son, Taylor, and his friends. Dallas, the beautiful ginger man, who came with him, ruined my plans. He'd made me question everything I'd thought I knew about myself.

Dallas

There were a lot of things on my to-do list. The main one was trying not to burn out while I worked full-time and prepared for my last year of college. What hadn't made it to my list was walking in on one of my friend's fathers naked. Lee Porter intrigued me. When I returned home, a chance encounter brought us back together. Fascination turned to something else, and I was going to make the older man mine.

1

DALLAS

The scenery was beautiful as I made my way through the backroads and enjoyed being away from the city. When my lifelong best friend, Carolyn, told me to come along with her and her boyfriend, Taylor, on a week's stay at his family lake house, I'd jumped at the chance. I couldn't exactly afford spring break like the rest of my friends. Carolyn knew it, and while I wanted to be a little pissed about her arranging this trip because it wouldn't cost me anything, I needed it too much. I'd had to pull doubles at my already full-time job on top of school just to get the time off. My boss was great, and he'd paid his way through college, so he let me work extra so I wouldn't miss out on my money. Even one missed paycheck or week of tips would ruin everything I'd worked for.

I was in my junior year of college, and pretty much every dime I made went into paying my bills and covering my tuition. My parents had refused to help in any way because I hadn't submitted to what they wanted from me. The last time I'd gone home for the summer was during my freshman year, and they'd tried to convince me to be the good obedient son. When I'd left to return to school, they'd told me not to call for help unless I planned to come home. Only to get a call a few months later summoning me for the holidays. Their overbearing ways weren't the only reason I didn't want to return to the fold.

The minute I'd driven back to the apartment my best friend had found for us, I swore I'd make it on my own no matter what it took. That's why I was always on the edge of exhaustion and burnout, but I was too stubborn to ask for help. I wouldn't prove my parents right by failing.

The GPS on my phone told me my turn was coming up. I was about an hour ahead of Carolyn and Taylor. They'd still been in bed when I tried to get them up. So I told them I was heading out, and Taylor had thrown the key at me and told me to just let myself in.

I'd stopped to pick up groceries and some beer and liquor. They said they'd pay me back when they arrived. I turned off onto a long winding driveway, disappearing into the trees and my eyes widened as I pulled up to a beautiful home with a garage. The house was right on the lake, and as I parked, I turned off the engine and heard nothing but nature sounds and peace.

Fuck, I'd needed that.

I jumped out of my car, crossed the yard, and jogged up the steps to unlock the deadbolt. I entered, closed the door, looked around, and set the keys on an end table. It almost looked like something out of a magazine. I'd never say it out loud, but I almost regretted that I wouldn't have the place to myself.

"Who the hell are you?" a deep, gravelly voice asked from behind me, and I spun.

Shit, a massive man stood there naked, and my eyes dropped involuntarily to his crotch. A thick bush of pubes was at the base of a long, slender dick. Fuck, I slammed my eyes closed before I did something stupid and pivoted so fast I made myself dizzy.

"Um, shit, um, I'm Dallas." The vision of the burly, hairy man was burned on the backs of my eyelids. I'd never be able to look at the man ever again.

"Am I supposed to know you?"

"I'm Carolyn's best friend."

"My son's girlfriend?" he asked, and something in his tone made my once tense shoulders relax but not completely.

"Yes," I practically screamed. I wasn't a small guy, I was six-one and leanly muscled, but I totally didn't see myself beating the guy behind me in a fight. I was a natural pacifist. That macho bullshit had passed me by.

"You can turn around."

"No, that's okay, I'm fine." I almost glanced behind me as a gruff chuckle filled with amusement shocked me, and then I heard heavy steps moving away. Pushing a relieved sigh between my compressed lips that puffed out my cheeks, I relaxed completely—nearly sagging against the back of the sectional sofa. Taylor hadn't talked much about his dad, just said the man had separated from his husband and the divorce recently became final.

"It's safe now," he said as I carefully turned around to find him in a pair of jeans and pulling a t-shirt to cover his extremely hairy upper body. "Now, why are you here?"

"Taylor and Carolyn are about an hour behind me, or at least that's what they told me. He invited us to spend our spring break here," I explained and saw no recognition on his face. Shit, my plans seemed to be falling through.

"Of course he did," he muttered under his breath.

"Should I leave?" I was waiting for the disappointment to hit me as a well-needed vacation was quickly slipping through my fingers the longer I stood there.

He gave a shake of his head and gave me a friendly smile. "No, he told me he was staying in the city last time we talked. I was just expecting to have the place to myself for another week until I went back to the city."

"I can leave. It's not a big deal." I hoped I didn't sound as disappointed as I felt.

"No, you got stuff to bring in?" He gave me another comforting smile and waved off my offer to leave.

"Um, yeah, I stopped and got some groceries and stuff. Since I'm the only one who cooks, they put me in charge."

"I'm Lee Porter." He approached me and stretched out his arm. I briefly shook his hand and was surprised by the slight callouses on the pads of his fingers.

"As I said, I'm Dallas. I can get everything."

"No need, I'll help."

I nearly threw a tantrum but held it in as I left the house with him behind me. Leaning into the open driver's side window, I popped the trunk. I hadn't known if I'd take the long way to the house so I'd stowed the perishable items in an ice-filled cooler. I slipped on my hiking pack, which was all I had in the way of luggage. To be honest, with careful folding, every-thing I owned could've fit in that pack. Lee grabbed the cooler while I picked up the two oversized reusable shopping bags.

I followed behind him and made a note to text Carolyn and tell her about my newest awkward situation. The last good one was going home for summer break at the end of my freshman year to walk in on my girlfriend getting spit-roasted by my older twin brothers. She'd only stopped long enough to ask me to join. I hadn't been home since, just another reason to never go back to my small hometown. I was not looking my pastor father in the eyes and explaining why I kept making excuses to *never* visit again. There were more reasons than my ex-girlfriend fucking my brothers while I was away, but it was the perfect excuse instead of dwelling on how much of a disappointment I was. I mentally shook off the thoughts because they never got me anywhere good for my peace of mind.

When we entered the kitchen, I fell in love. One of the things I valued more than anything was cooking, and that room was a dream come true for me. I lifted the bags onto the counter.

"You got a lot," he commented.

"I like to cook," I said as I slipped the straps off my shoulders and leaned my pack against the wall.

"I knew it wasn't for my son or Carolyn. His delivery spending is killing me."

I smiled as he winked at me. "I work nights, so I'm not home to cook for them."

"You live with him? I don't think he mentioned a new roommate."

"No, Carolyn and I are roommates, but Taylor might as well be a third roommate. Not that I don't like him being around." I rushed to explain in an attempt not to offend him.

"Relax," he said as he started emptying the items in the cooler into the fridge and freezer. I asked him where to put the pantry stuff, and he pointed toward a cabinet near the stainless steel fridge. "I lived with the kid for eighteen years. I know how annoying he can be."

Quickly, everything was put away, and I was awkward about what to do or say. I didn't always do well with strangers in certain situations that required small talk. I was one of the weird pastor's kids who grew up with strict rules and spent all our free time in church with very little socialization. We'd been preached to daily about the evils of the world outside our church, which made my modest girlfriend and my brothers' threesome incident that much more awkward.

Although, I was a normal man who loved sex and who'd been active since I was sixteen, so I wasn't a prude. I'd just never tried with the girlfriend because my parents had picked her. They said she'd make a good preacher's wife, which they'd decided was going to be my life's calling. Not even close.

"Grab your bag. I'll take you to the guest room and show you where everything is." He circled the island, and I picked up my bag to follow him through the house. He showed me where the guest bathroom was, Taylor's room, and finally opened the shut door across from my friend's. "This one is yours. Mine is at the end of the hall. Sometimes it gets chilly at night, there's extra blankets in the hall closet and more towels. If you need anything until Taylor and Carolyn get here, I'll be in the living room."

"I'm probably going to crash for a few hours. I worked a double yesterday to finish getting the week off."

"Have a good nap." He left me to get settled.

I closed the door, dropped my pack in front of the dresser, and dragged my feet to the bed. Kicking off my sneakers, I fell face-first onto the bed. I had about a week of sleep to catch up on. I was looking forward to being done with that school year, and all I'd have to worry about was work. I couldn't forget saving for my senior year tuition. I loved my job, even though I knew I complained about it a lot. But I was looking forward to no school and only a job to worry about.

I crossed my arms under my head and buried my face in them to block out the bright sunlight. My friends would wake me up when they got there. Until then, I was going to enjoy not having to set the alarm and drinking lethal amounts of coffee to get through my day.

2

LEE

I shook my head and tried to suppress my smile, remembering the kid's face when he turned around earlier to find himself faced with a grumpy naked man. That had been a few hours ago, and the amusement still hadn't worn off. The house was supposed to be all mine for two weeks. I'd invited Taylor, but he'd said he was going to stay in the city with his friends. I knew it was to give me space after Roger and I had signed the final divorce papers.

After ten years of marriage, but fifteen together, I'd walked in on him fucking our business partner of a year over his desk. He'd tried to say that his cheating was a one-time thing, but I'd laughed in his face. We'd had an open relationship the entire time we were together, so it wasn't like he had to lie to me. The only stipulation we'd agreed on was that we told each other if we were interested in someone and were in a sexual relationship with them. I'd thought about letting it go, and then the thought popped into my head about how many others he hadn't told me about. I'd never gone without a condom, even with my husband, and I felt thankful for that. He hadn't seemed to be too discriminating or even respectful of my safety.

Then before I could call the marriage quits, he'd asked for the divorce to have a monogamous relationship with said business partner.

My forty-two-year-old self had asked why him and not me. I'd brought up the not seeing other people several times, and he'd said no. That stung the pride and ego, but it was fine, I got the lake house, and he got our home in the city. They had to buy me out of my part of the club. Which left me with plenty of money, enough that I wouldn't have to rush to find another job for a while. Although, a friend of mine was losing his long-time business partner and asked me to buy in. My friend couldn't buy the partner out. The investment was a smart move since the pub had been going for seventeen years with steady growth. College cities were good for bars and clubs.

The door opening made me turn my head to find my son and his girlfriend coming in.

"Surprise!" My adorable, blond, blue-eyed son grinned at me. I wouldn't deny I'd spoiled the kid rotten. I'd been a single dad until he was five.

"Not as much as your friend. He got a nice view of a naked, excessively hairy man." The mental image of his expression made me smile. But for a second, before I realized he was a friend of my son's, I'd wondered if he'd liked what he saw. He'd definitely dropped his gaze right before he'd spun away from me.

Taylor and Carolyn laughed so hard they choked. They tossed their bags aside and ran to the couch to curl up against my sides, and I wrapped my arms around them.

"What's with this visit?"

"You don't want us here?" he asked, and I rolled my eyes as they both batted their eyes at me. My son and his girlfriend were made for each other. I'd adored her from the second I met her, especially because she made my son happy.

"Shut up, yes. But you didn't call to tell me." I brushed a kiss to her forehead and then his.

"We were going to stay with Dallas, but then I thought we could come here instead."

"Dallas was going to work his entire break, and I didn't want him alone. He hasn't had one vacation in three years." Carolyn had an odd tone in her voice. There was a story there, and after meeting him, I'd admit to a bit of curiosity about who the young man was.

"No family to go home to?" I asked.

"He has them, but picture this, after you go home for the summer freshman year, well, finding your supposed girlfriend spit-roasted between your older brothers in your bed no less, you'd probably decide less time at home would be good."

"You're fucking lying." Poor kid. I knew what it was like to walk in on a cheating partner.

She shook her head. "And his family is ultra-conservative, pastor dad, stereotypical preacher's wife mom and trying to push you to get married during every phone call. They wanted him to go to seminary to follow in the family tradition of leading his own church. So they won't help out with college because it doesn't align with their values. Instead, he's killing himself with a full-time job, twice-monthly plasma donations, and a heavy load at school."

"Poor kid. How did you two meet?" They seemed close for just meeting in college. Most of my college friends lost contact after we'd graduated. We'd run into each other in the city a few times, but it was just a quick, polite conversation and then moving on in our separate directions.

"Kindergarten. He's like a brother, and I couldn't bear to be separated from him. Yet I also feel like a bitch because I can't be without him."

"He looks like a good kid." I kept calling him a kid, but he looked like anything but one. Over six feet of lean, gorgeous young man with pretty ginger hair and a dusting of scruff. I'd hated that I'd noticed. Dirty old man came to mind, but I had an extremely healthy sex drive, and it'd been over a year since I'd gotten laid. Good thing the young man was straight. It would keep me from flirting...maybe.

"He is. So we arranged this, but he still worked his ass off at the restaurant for two weeks to make sure he didn't mess up his money situation. He just has to make it until summer break and then just working will be like a vacation."

"You were nice, weren't you, Dad?"

"Yes, I was nice. I'm always nice." And that was true. Despite my looks, I was always the nice guy. People looked at me with the heavy sideburns, crazy facial hair, put that on top of the body, the hair, and the belly, and I didn't usually instill comfort in people. To be honest, I'd started to feel my age a few years ago and had started to cut down on my regularly sched-uled weekly hookups from a long list of old friends. I'd never been one to take a stranger home. I required at least a small connection with someone I went to bed with.

"Except assaulting him with your hatred of clothes." Taylor poked my belly, and I growled at him.

"If I was informed that I'd have guests that weren't of the nudist variety, I would've been dressed, so that's all your fault... not mine."

"Okay, I'll accept that one. Is Dallas taking a nap?" Taylor asked.

"I haven't heard movement from the guest room in a few hours. You're late getting here."

"We didn't want to get out of bed. There was a huge party last night, and we didn't fall into bed until dawn." Carolyn once again batted her lashes.

"Of course, the perks of being carefree students. Talking

about that, Taylor, we have to have a discussion about your delivery this year. You're going to break me." He rolled his eyes knowing that I wouldn't cut him off for anything. My parents had done that when I'd come out.

"It's better when Dallas can cook for us. Speaking of which, did you see a receipt for whatever he bought?" he asked.

"Not that I noticed, but he stocked up. I'll pay for whatever he bought. Just find out how much."

"Great, we figured if he cooked, we'd make a deal that we'd pay for everything he bought. He'll fight us, but I haven't lost to him yet. I'm going to bounce on him." She quickly kissed my scruffy cheek and jumped off the couch to take off running.

"Should I be worried?" I asked.

"You know I'm like you, I don't get jealous, and I trust my girlfriend. But no, Dallas and her are like annoying siblings with each other."

"Dammit, Carolyn," Dallas shouted from down the hall.

"Well, maybe I shouldn't worry about your relationship, but is his safety in question?"

"Maybe some bruises."

He leaned back into my side, and I was lucky that my son wasn't afraid of still receiving affection from his parents. I'd worried as he'd grown and realized what some people thought about kids with gay parents that he'd put distance between us. Terror at him being bullied and all had kept me up nights, and then I got a call from school about my son being in a fight when someone had been homophobic about him having two dads. That had been the first and last time anyone openly commented.

"Have you talked to your Pop?" I asked.

"No."

"Taylor, he helped raise you. I don't want this shit to ruin your relationship with him." Roger had been a great stepdad and accepted my son when I told him that I'd been in a relationship with a woman in my late teens to early twenties. I'd worried about dating as a single, gay dad. The unplanned pregnancy resulted in me being a full-time parent and my ex-girlfriend being a great mother figure and friend to Taylor.

"No, he did that. He fucked around on you. I wasn't stupid not to notice the other men you and him brought home to the *private rooms* in the guest house growing up, and then when you explained it and your agreement, if he'd been honest, I'd be okay, but he lied his ass off."

"We all make mistakes, honey. Your pop is no different." I'd made a promise to never badmouth Roger because despite what happened, we'd had a good marriage until those last few years.

"Maybe, but I'm just not ready yet."

"That's fine, but don't completely cut him off. He was your other parent for fifteen years. After things cool off, maybe call him." He nodded in answer but didn't say anything else.

We sat there listening to the muffled conversation, and I flipped through channels until Carolyn and Dallas were ready to come out of the room. I'd wanted the quiet time. Yet I was happy my son was there. We spent a good amount of time together, but with school and friends, we shared phone calls or texts more than him visiting. Although, I'd been in transition the past year and decided against finding a place until I figured out what I was going to do with my life. Once I returned home, I'd see about restarting my life which had stalled since the separation. I was only forty-two. I wasn't fucking dead yet.

3
DALLAS

The first official morning of vacation, and I was stalking the coffeemaker waiting for it to finish brewing. It was nine AM, but I'd been up since eight trying to talk myself into going back to sleep. That had been a no-go, and I finally got up feeling frustrated with my lack of ability to be lazy. Also, Carolyn and I had a disagreement about paying for all the groceries, and I hated fighting with her. Lee said he'd pay for everything since I was taking over the cooking. Cost of food for labor, so I'd reluctantly agreed. I didn't like being the poor kid who had to worry that groceries would break me.

"Aren't college students supposed to drag ass out of bed at like noon?" Lee asked from behind me, and I started to turn, only to freeze.

He chuckled, and I rolled my eyes. People loved to laugh at me. "I have pants on. I knew there were other people in the house," he said as I heard his bare feet shuffle on the tile floor and the fridge opening. "You're shit out of luck about a shirt, though."

I glanced over my shoulder to notice dark blond hair spread over his shoulders and upper back in varying degrees of thickness. His skin was pale, but I remembered Taylor had mentioned his dads had owned a club in the city and were mostly night people. He pulled out a bottle of creamer.

"Taylor said you were a night person. I wasn't expecting anyone to be up." I had to admit I liked a quiet in the morning before the chaos of my day started. Sometimes I felt like an old man trapped in a twenty-two-year-old body. No one else my age had to deal with the bullshit I did, or at least I hadn't met anyone like me.

"Since I was bought out of the club with the divorce, my sleep habits changed."

"Do you want breakfast?" I felt restless and unable to relax. I knew I was used to working, but being there with my friend's dad, for some reason, I felt as if I needed to pay for my stay there.

"Babe, sit down and enjoy your coffee. You're not here to work. Unless you're hungry, you don't have to cook. Enjoy your vacation." He came up beside me, set the creamer down, and then grabbed two mugs from the cabinet over the coffeemaker. "Just plan to make something when Taylor and Carolyn get up."

"I don't know what to do," I muttered.

"Carolyn said you work all the time when you're not in school."

"My grades were good but not enough for a scholarship to the school Carolyn was accepted to. I qualified for some grants that covered books and a part of my tuition." Before I could reach for the carafe, he grabbed it and filled both mugs. He asked how I liked my coffee, and as I answered, he made it for me. I was speechless for a minute and then finished my thought. "The rest I have to make. I don't want to take on the debt of student loans."

"What are you going to school for?" he asked as he picked

up the mugs and moved them to the island. He pulled out the barstool at the end and motioned me to sit down.

"Business degree. I want to open my own restaurant one day. The chef where I work has been training me on the job, but I may need to go to culinary school...he said with my skills, I wouldn't need it, but..." I sat on the stool, and he took the right one directly beside me. Had the man not heard of personal space, there was an entire island, two other stools.

"You're still uncomfortable about knowing enough to handle the kitchen as the head chef."

"Yeah, that. Taylor said you ran a club with your ex." I changed the subject. I hated talking about myself, and sensed Lee had a more interesting life.

"Yeah, we bought it about ten years ago. The owner was about to go bankrupt and just wanted out. I worked security there...still did until Roger and I broke up. Roger was the bar manager. We pooled what we had and came up with enough to have collateral for a loan. Took a few years to turn everything around. Poor business management by the former owner was slow to turn around. We pretty much bought his debt. It was a mess."

"Why didn't you keep the club? You sound like you were successful at it."

"Roger fucked our business partner and lied about it. I didn't want to stay in the business with them. But a few months ago, a friend approached me about buying into his pub near the college. He doesn't have the funds to buy out his business partner, and being debt-free, he'd like to stay that way. But his partner wants to leave and asked if I wanted to make the investment. It would be a bit of a break. Huge difference between the vibe of a massive dance club and a neighborhood pub."

"Do you want a break?"

He smiled and then sipped his coffee as if he were thinking about it. "I don't know," he said quietly as he set the mug down. "Don't get me wrong, no seven days a week, twelve hours a day in a loud, packed club. Be kinda nice, I think. That's been my life outside of taking care of Taylor for years. What about you? Looking forward to school being over soon for the summer?"

I shrugged my shoulders and scraped my short thumbnail along the side of the mug. "I don't know, like it would be nice, to not leave school, go to work, get home to sleep, get up and repeat every day. Look at me. I woke up at eight AM on my vacation because my brain said I should be doing something. I'm in the kitchen three nights, and the other two, I'm tending bar and volunteering for shifts where they're available."

"And the rest of the time you're in school?" I nodded and glanced at him. "You're what, twenty-one, two?"

"Twenty-two."

"You have to take time, babe. You have the rest of your life to wear yourself out." I started to protest, but he held up his hand. "But I understand. School isn't cheap, especially when you're doing it by yourself. Take the week to relax. I'll even remind you whenever you need it. Recharge." He winked at me over the rim of his mug as he raised it to his lips for another sip.

"Easier said than done."

"True. Okay, I'm going to check to make sure the boat is fueled up. We're going out when the other two wake up, and we'll have lunch at this funky place farther up the lake that sells really good barbecue. My treat, and then you can make something for dinner."

I nodded as he finished off his coffee then he slipped off the stool. I watched him leave through the sliding glass door that led to the back deck. We'd sat out there last night having beers and talking. I'd made flatbread pizzas because everyone wanted something quick, or they just didn't want me in the kitchen.

Carolyn and Taylor were forever fussing at me to take a breath, but I was worried about everything. I felt as if I had no control over anything in my life. Going home was a no because as much as people wanted to think it was to avoid my ex, but honestly, I'd never fit. Taking a vacation without nearly killing myself was impossible until I was done with school. And then, when school was over, what was I going to do for a job? My boss already said I could start full-time after I graduated. I just wanted control of one thing in my life.

Which at this point seemed unattainable, but I guess I could start small and try to enjoy my first time away in years. Lee said he'd remind me. Maybe that was something I needed. I was sick of being exhausted all the time. Tired of being the person who had to turn down every invite to hang out with my friends because I had to work. Only one more year, and I'd be able to walk across that stage. I'd leave school with no debt and be able to go on with a real life. I just had to be patient.

4
LEE

Jesus fucking Christ.

I hated my life at that moment. Three days in Dallas's presence and everything I swore I wouldn't do, I was doing. I was hiding my eyes behind dark sunglasses as Dallas, Taylor, and Carolyn were spread out on the dock taking in the bright afternoon sun. Dallas's freckled skin was taking on a light tan that surprised me when it came to him being a ginger, but Carolyn was obsessed with covering him with sunscreen almost every hour on the hour. A body that was almost completely smooth except for a thick treasure trail, and I was too intent on finding out where that line of hair led.

Years of working in a club, I saw young dancers practically naked except for tight shorts, and the patrons weren't much better—a lot of leather and latex. I'd thought I was immune. Well, I wasn't, but what bothered me the most was I'd never fallen for the sex appeal of a younger man before and never a straight man.

Too much experience in dealing with homophobic men, but if my son even caught a hint of bigotry in someone, he wouldn't put up with it. Dallas seemed like a genuinely nice guy, put too much pressure on himself, and was headed toward a burnout of epic proportions. Because I liked to take care of things, remove stress from friends, my brain was trying to figure out how to help. Yet he was my son's friend, not mine, and I'd completely overstep if I did more than try to pull him out of thinking about work while he was there.

I jerked my attention out to the water as Taylor and Carolyn jumped up, and they cannonballed into the slightly choppy surface of the lake. Dallas yelled as they soaked his front, and he got to his feet. His tiny swim shorts were wet. The fabric clung to a sizable bulge, and I realized I wasn't going to survive the damn vacation. I was a grown-ass man, but I wasn't afraid to admit to at least myself that I wanted to run scared. Go back to the city to let them have the house to themselves. I breathed out a sigh of relief as he dove in to join his friends.

I was two decades older than Dallas. And while I had no issues with my body, I was showing my years. My body hair became thicker with every birthday. The curve of my belly was rounder. I'd never been the type to go for a younger man. I tended to hook up with men closer to my age or older. My ex-husband was only a few years older than me. I think the fact that I wasn't comfortable dating men who were my son's age made me less apt to do the middle-aged man thing. I'd even given Taylor a lecture about being cautious around older men who may not respect him and just want to fuck him. Currently, I was feeling more than a bit hypocritical.

I found Dallas beautiful, but he was also smart, ambitious, and had his shit together, already so sure of what he wanted from life. At twenty-two, I was just trying to figure out what I needed to do—how to raise my son on my own. Taria had helped, stayed at my apartment at night to watch over Taylor, and took care of her homework in her first few years of medical school.

To be honest, I didn't know what I would've done without her. I'd loved my girlfriend. Being with her wasn't some traumatizing or painful experience. I hadn't even found any faults in our sexual life, except that I wasn't completely satisfied with the physical aspect. That didn't mean I regretted our relationship.

Attraction had never been something shameful for me. I'd check out men, and if I wanted to take them home or go to their place, or in some cases a motel, I'd never hesitated. What consenting adults did together shouldn't be a negative experience. It's why the open relationship and then marriage, I'd embraced sex positivity and made up for my time in the closet, ignoring the shame my family tried to place on me.

Yet, I was a bit ashamed of my reaction to Dallas, and once I returned to the city, my attraction to Dallas would just be a pleasant memory. Something to remind me that the past year hadn't destroyed my needs and wants. I pushed up from my chair, headed toward the dock, and dove in to spend some time with my son because I hadn't been able to do that enough.

I DRANK A BEER SITTING ON ONE OF THE CHAIRS BESIDE THE LAKE, THE kids were inside watching a movie, but I'd made an excuse to have some quiet time. All day and through the evening, I'd studied everything about the young man. In the short time together, I'd learned he was at his most relaxed in the kitchen. He kept up a steady stream of conversation as he expertly prepared every meal with so much passion and love.

You could see how important food was to him, especially

the interaction over the meal. There was no rush to finish eating. He savored every bite and looked so proud seeing how we enjoyed the food he'd prepared.

"You mind some company?" Dallas asked, and I tipped my head back to find his shadowed figure.

"No. Thought you and the kids were having some cheesy creature feature marathon."

"We were, but as much as I love Carolyn and Taylor, some-times it feels like I'm the third wheel," he said as he sat down beside me and leaned his head back. "Thanks for letting us crash your vacation."

"No need for that. I don't get to see Taylor enough. He has school and his friends. I had work and Roger and then dealing with all the divorce stuff. Your cooking has more than paid me back for crashing my vacation, as you said."

"Thanks. I always loved to cook. Before I left my hometown, I worked at one of the nicer places in our town. Mostly as a server, but occasionally the chef would let me observe, but he wasn't one to let you help if you weren't up to his standard."

"How did you get the job at your current place?" I wanted to know more about him. What would be the harm in shared conversation while we were together?

"I showed up to apply. They promoted from within, which meant I had to start at the bottom with dishwashing and bussing tables. When they were short-staffed, the chef needed help with prep, so I'd volunteered. I was moved to the front of the house and worked as a server. One night my sophomore year, I asked if I could start training for one of the assistants or sous chef positions. I was shocked that the chef said yes. My boss knew I was paying for college, so he asked if I wanted to train for a part-time bartending slot that had opened up."

"Well, you definitely have amazing skills. I haven't found anything of yours I haven't liked. And I've spent a lot of time in restaurants. Many of my friends are in the food and bar industry, comes with the territory. I know you don't have much time, but is there anything you do for fun?" I turned my head to find him staring off into space as if he were thinking about it. He had a strong profile. A proud tilt to his chin, and against my better judgment, I liked him.

"Nothing much, actually. I'm boring. When I'm not dealing with school and work, I tend to like my quiet...maybe catch up on my sleep that I'm always lacking. What about you?"

"Beautiful men." I smiled as he snorted. "I was in the closet until I was almost your age, so I did some making up for lost time."

"Were you happy with your girlfriend?"

"Yes, I loved her. We had a great relationship in every way. While the sex wasn't perfect, I was in my late teens and twenties, sex was great no matter what. You have a girlfriend?"

"No."

"Why is that, besides lack of time?"

"Um, I don't know. I dated my high school girlfriend for three years, our parents were even planning the wedding, but I didn't want to marry her. Freshman year, I was trying to figure out a way to break up with her. My brothers just gave me the excuse."

"Carolyn mentioned you walking in on her and them."

His rich laughter sent a shiver up my spine, and I felt the ache of need that I'd never be able to entertain. "That was something I didn't need to see. We talked, and she wasn't in any more of a hurry to marry me than I was her. Last I heard, she's engaged to one of them. She's living with *them*. I'm just wondering how long before my parents figure it out that they're a very happy throuple. I may not go home, but I still get gossip from friends I had there, and Carolyn gets bits and pieces."

I chuckled at the amusement in his voice. "But that doesn't explain why you don't have one now?"

"I'm more hookups when time permits. Quick fucks to take the edge off the stress. Don't say anything, but as much as I seem the king of the one-night stand, I'm the monogamous type. It's just..."

"Just what?"

"Right now, it wouldn't be fair to a girlfriend to have her importance ranked behind work and school. I figured once I graduate, I can give finding a relationship more priority. Have you dated since your divorce? You can tell me it's none of my business if you want."

"I have no issue with questions. I'm a pretty brutally honest person." I grimaced because I was not being honest, but it was hopeless. "No, I have a long list of friends with benefits, and despite my open marriage, I'd started getting a bit...burned out and suggested we close the relationship. Roger wasn't interested, and it didn't bother me enough to fight him on it."

"But didn't you get jealous?"

That was a question I got a lot, but I'd never found myself jealous in romantic relationships. I experienced envy over monogamous couples. The arrangement just worked for Roger and me. "No. To me, jealousy is a trust issue, and I trusted Roger. Seems more than I should have. With everything final now, maybe it's time to get back out there. First, though, I texted my friend about buying out his business partner and scheduled a meeting." I wasn't the type of person to just sit around. And while I could probably make my money last, I was forty-two, and for me, that was way too early for retirement.

"You said the pub would be a break from the club."

"It will. I kinda think it'll be a nice change."

We talked well into the early hours after midnight. The night was nice. He'd asked questions, and I had, too. I enjoyed my time with him. I experienced a certain sadness with the thought I'd probably never see him again. Earlier I'd decided that would be best, but the longer I spent with him, the less I wanted to break contact. And because of that, I needed to keep my distance, or I was going to do something that would hurt everyone involved.

5

DALLAS

I'd been sorry to see my week at the lake end, but I was glad to be home and back to my routine. Lee had spent most of the week giving me gentle reminders to relax, and while I'd listened, it hadn't been easy. School was almost out and then I would be back to just dealing with work, yet I still felt restless for some reason.

Every time I slowed down, my brain would go back to the lake house. The peace I'd found there, just being able to be without all the pressure I put on myself stripped away months and years of constant anxiety. I figured that was what was going on. Yet, that also didn't seem right. After shoving my black dress shirt into my bag, I sighed heavily as I slung the strap of my backpack over one shoulder. I combed my fingers through my hair and loosened the product I used to tame the waves. The night was a bit muggy, and my skin exposed by my tank felt sweaty and uncomfortable.

Normally I drove during the school year, but when I was feeling a bit off, I enjoyed a walk to decompress before heading home. At least my friends wouldn't expect me at a certain time. Carolyn wasn't a fan of me walking so late, but it was only

thirty minutes to our apartment building. Also, with it being a
college town and a Friday night, the streets in the bar and club
district near campus were packed with people.

I started to think about grabbing dinner—stop to get a
greasy burger and fries. I rarely indulged to save money and
usually put an order in before the kitchen closed. We were
provided two free meals during our shifts, which we could take
home if we wanted. But since I'd felt weird, I'd forgotten about
it until the kitchen crew shut everything down. We closed at
midnight every day, and we were closed on Mondays.

Fuck it, there was a diner on the way home. I'd get something to go and eat in front of the TV after a long hot shower. I
took in my surroundings. Moving to the city after living in a
small town had been a culture shock, but I didn't know if I
could handle the laidback pace of my hometown after living in
the city for years. Public transport to save money when needed.
Plenty of opportunities for jobs in my chosen profession after
graduation. There I could pretend I wasn't a socially awkward
preacher's kid, the youngest of three, and a disappointment.

The thought bothered me. I'd done everything right.
Worked a job as soon as I could get one. Busted my ass in
school, but I wasn't a straight-A student like my brothers. I
didn't play a sport while my brothers were stars on the football
team. I'd never measured up, and not having those mistakes
pointed out at every opportunity felt good.

That didn't mean I hadn't searched for that place to belong.
I'd sort of found it at my job. I was an A and B college student,
and I already had my future planned out. I felt confident I was
doing all the right things. That's why the restlessness like I was
missing something annoyed me.

I grunted as a broad body collided with me, and strong arms
went around my waist. "I'm sorry, honey, Dallas, hey."

I slightly tipped my head back to look up at Lee smiling at

me. He seemed to be making sure I was steady and then released me. "Hey, what are you doing over this way?"

"Just finished my final meeting to sign the papers and make a cringe-worthy money transfer. You just getting off work?"

"Yeah, we were kinda slow. I got out right at midnight because we worked together to get all the side work done for the morning shift. Should I congratulate you or console you about buyer's regret?" I smiled as he chuckled and shook his head.

"A congratulations would be nice."

I didn't understand why I liked his smile so much or why the gruffness of his voice caused me to relax. My shoulders fell from their clenched shrug, and as if it hadn't existed at all, all my problems faded away. "Then congratulations."

"Thank you. Where are you headed?"

"You're welcome." A few excuse mes made me step out of the way of foot traffic, and then I answered him. "Actually, there's a diner on my way home, and I was thinking of getting a greasy, double bacon cheeseburger and fries."

"You just left a restaurant."

"I know, but I didn't remember to get my order in before they started cleaning the kitchen, and I wasn't taking my life in my hands by delaying them."

"Those kitchen crews are scary."

"Very. And also, it rarely happens, but I didn't feel like going home to cook, and I think we're out of sandwich stuff."

"You mind if I walk with you?"

"No." He nodded and turned to walk beside me as we made our way toward the diner. "Looking forward to getting back to work?"

"Actually, I already started. When I returned, we had a meeting. They gave me access to all the financial information and books, and I started going in during the evenings to observe. We negotiated back and forth for a few weeks until we agreed on a fair price."

"What did you observe?" I didn't know why but I loved the sound of his voice. There was a soothing quality to the gruff tone that made it feel as if all my worries and tension didn't exist. With him, he had no expectations of me or would try to convince me to do something different to make my way through college. I was simply able to be.

"Staff and customer interactions. Looked for any security issues. They only have one person at the door checking IDs which is required in a college city, but I'd like to see one more bouncer at least on weekends when the kids start coming in. Made sure the bartenders and the bar-backs didn't heavy pour and knew when to cut someone off. Also, that they didn't make a habit of favoring something pretty." I chuckled. "Studied the menu and sampled the food. Nothing as good as your cooking, but it's a pub with bar fare."

I was a bit uncomfortable with the compliment but pushed it aside to focus on him. "Everything seemed to work out if you bought in."

"Yeah, there's a few things, but I'll talk to Tom more about that. I know how to run a club. Pub environments and vibes are definitely different. They have a very relaxed atmosphere and a lot of regulars."

"What does being one of the owners entail?"

"Actually, extremely cushy, weeks are alternated, one week I'd cover days and the next I'd take nights. They typically want an owner/manager on-premise, but that's not a steadfast rule. He's built a competent staff. They all seem to know their jobs and don't have a lot of turnover in employees. But now the real work starts."

"What's that?" I asked as I turned to take in his profile, and he seemed happier and more relaxed than he had even been at the lake.

"Settling into my new place. I'd rented a small corporate apartment while I was in the holding pattern of what I was going to do. There was this great two-bedroom loft apartment my real estate agent found me that I couldn't pass up. But I loathe shopping."

"Well, you're a bachelor now. What do you really need? A bed, couch, and TV." I teased him, and he glanced at me, and our gazes met, but I looked away too quickly.

"That would've worked when I was your age, but as I, grown-ass man in my forties, I think I should upgrade."

"Boring." I sighed heavily and caused him to laugh, and I was shocked again that I really liked the timbre of it. It was warm and gruff, and I frowned but shook it off.

"I know, that's me, the middle-aged, divorced man. I'm hopeless."

"Yeah, yeah, here's the diner. I was just going to get something to go and then head home."

"Then I'll let you get to it. It was nice to see you again, Dallas."

"It was."

"Give me your phone." I didn't even question why. I just pulled it from my pocket, unlocked it, and handed it over. He tapped on the screen and handed it back. "There's my number. If you ever have a night off, give me a call, and I'll buy you a drink. I enjoyed our talks, tonight and at the lake house."

"I'll do that. Be safe going home."

"You, too." He seemed to want to say something else but looked away. "Why don't you text me when you get home just so I know you got there?"

"Okay." We said our goodbyes and I turned to watch him go back the way we came. I opened my mouth to ask if I could buy him dinner but clenched my teeth because I noticed something I shouldn't. I was taking in the way his shirt stretched across his broad shoulders and back, and his hair was just touching the neckline. Jeans that skimmed his long thick legs.

The restlessness I'd experienced for weeks suddenly returned, and I realized it had disappeared the second I heard his voice. What the fuck was wrong with me? I shook it off. He'd become almost like a friend during the time I'd spent at his house. He'd made sure I relaxed but never lectured me on maybe cutting down on work or applying for a loan or deferring a year to save up. Lee didn't make me feel as if my decisions were detrimental just because it didn't allow me to have some superficial social life.

I entered the diner and stepped up to the counter. As if on autopilot, I ordered the food I was craving and added a large milkshake. I just needed sleep and maybe making a new friend wasn't a bad thing, especially one who got me and my goals.

6

LEE

Goddamn, I hissed through my teeth as I worked my cock through my fist and my ass clenched around my plug. In my head, a beautiful ginger-haired man was heavy between my thighs as he fucked me into the mattress. Dallas's smooth body covered in sweat as he stared down at me, his face flushed. I tried to imagine the feel of him when I'd grabbed him a week earlier when we ran into each other.

"Come on, baby, you know you wanna come all over Daddy's cock," his smooth baritone whispered as fantasy Dallas fucked me.

He lowered until his lips almost touched mine, but my brain wouldn't break that barrier. No one I'd ever been with had been a kisser. It had seemed too intimate with a casual hook-up since we'd always been in it for the fuck. I pushed the memories of everyone else aside. Only one man mattered. I squeezed around the toy buried in my clenching asshole and imagined it was Dallas inside me. Because of my looks, I'd defaulted to a top, but that wasn't what I wanted—not with him. Blood rushed in my ears, and I held my breath. I wanted it to last, but at the same time, I wanted to come. My strokes sped up until my back was arching and I shot my load, covering my hairy stomach. I laid there on my air mattress in the middle of my empty living room as I kept working my dick, not wanting it to end.

I cupped my furry sac and shoved the fingers of my free hand through my hair. Fuck, it was like I was in my early twenties again. Every evening and morning since I'd left him in front of the diner, I'd jerked off to what Dallas would do to me.

I reached for the towel I'd dropped beside the mattress after my shower the previous night. Quickly, I cleaned myself up and tossed the soiled fabric in the direction of my pile of dirty clothes. I relaxed as the bright late morning sun streamed around the edges of the blinds and added blackout curtains to the ever-growing list of shit I needed to get.

That day was all about furniture shopping and getting everything else I needed as well. The coming week would be my first at the pub. My professional life was shaping up, but the clusterfuck of my personal one wasn't looking so great. Why couldn't I forget him? I'd even pulled up several numbers of my friends with benefits, ones I knew who'd come through for me, but I'd tried, and all I'd succeeded in doing is feeling like shit.

Finding a fuck had never been an issue. Hell, I'd hooked up with at least one guy a week the entire time I was married. There wasn't any chance of anything happening. Yet I couldn't ignore the connection I felt to him. He made me feel so good. All the stress I carried over the separation, the divorce, all of it disappeared when I was with him. The way I was drawn to him terrified me because I knew there was no chance of me being able to do anything about it.

My phone beeped, and I grabbed it, unlocked it, and saw a text message from Dallas. Just seeing his name made my heart kick up in pace with excitement. I clicked on the message.

Dallas: *That drink still up for offer?*

My lips curled into a smile. He'd texted me to let me know

he'd gotten home, but no other messages since. I'd kind of given up on the hope he'd take me up on buying him a drink.

Lee: *Sure. Bad day?*

Dallas: *The roomie is abandoning me.*

Lee: *I feel special.*

Dallas: *You're not funny.*

Lee: *You busy today?*

Dallas: *No. Should I be suspicious?*

Lee: *Completely innocent.*

I combed my fingers through the hair on my chest and groaned as I realized my messages bordered on flirty. Hell, I couldn't remember the last time I flirted with a man at all.

Dallas: *I doubt that.*

He was right. I was naked in bed with a toy shoved up my ass. Damn glad he couldn't read minds. Could I be blamed, though? I hadn't gone without getting laid at least a few times a week in twenty years. A twelve-month dry spell was unnatural for me. Which made my reluctance to find someone weird.

Lee: *I'll give you that one. Wanna shop with me? After I'll buy you a drink and dinner.*

Dallas: *You haven't gotten furniture yet?*

Lee: *No, I need moral support. I can pout.*

Dallas: *Just be glad I sorta like you. When and where?*

I texted the address to a coffee place I liked and moaned with the shifting of the plug. My cock wanted to perk up, but my recovery time wasn't what it used to be.

Dallas: *I'll meet you at 11, but I require a massive coffee.*

Lee: *You name it, and it's yours.*

Dallas: *Don't tempt me. I'll see you soon.*

I was disappointed our conversation ended, but I'd see him soon. I struggled off the low mattress. In case he came home with me, I gathered all my suitcases and bags and shoved my dirty clothes into a laundry basket. Everything was stowed in what would be my bedroom in the upstairs loft. I didn't need a two-bedroom, but I'd picked a unit with a guest room. I'd also picked the one with the best kitchen—one that I didn't particularly need.

I rushed to get ready. I had an hour to get ready and then it was about half an hour to the coffee shop. Reminding myself that he was meeting me to hang out, it wasn't a date. That didn't mean I wasn't really looking forward to seeing him. I just had to behave, which I wasn't holding out much hope on.

"You're heading toward a tantrum," Dallas said with a chuckle behind me.

"I lived in the same house for fifteen years. I don't remember it being this much of a pain in the ass." I grumped as I kept trying to figure out which bed I wanted. We'd gone through and found everything else to fill my place with furniture. I just couldn't decide which bedroom suite to pick for my room. I'd gotten a bed and everything for the guest room.

He stepped up beside me, his shoulder bumping mine, and I glanced at him to find him smiling. He looked good in his t-shirt and slim-fit jeans that showed off his strong legs. When I'd met him earlier, I'd nearly leaned in to kiss his cheek, and I kept mentally screaming he was straight. Every part of me was ignoring the warnings of my brain. We'd grabbed an early lunch of sandwiches and coffee, but I'd get him something better for dinner.

"We've been shopping for two hours. You had no issues until this."

"I know."

"You know we still have to get sheets, towels, everything for your kitchen..."

"Hush, we're doing that shit online. We'll go to my place and pull out my laptop, and I'll buy you takeout."

"I'm an extremely expensive date." His baritone dipped low as he crowded my side, and I almost flinched.

"Good thing I'm not destitute. Which one do you like?" I asked.

"I like the simple one with the platform bed. You said your apartment was in an industrial-style building. Minimalist, I think you said."

"Yeah, I like the area, and it's near the pub. It's a two-bedroom loft. One bedroom and bathroom on the bottom, loft bedroom, and bathroom above. I liked the open space."

"The salesperson said if you pay in the next hour, they can do same-day delivery."

"I'll go with the one you picked."

"Good boy."

I slammed my eyes shut as he said that and was glad he was already moving away from me before I did something we'd both regret. He was driving me crazy, but I couldn't bear to end our day. The store had everything we needed, well, I needed, I had to stop saying we. I defaulted to we, such a couple thing to think, but we'd never be together—not even a casual hook-up to get off.

Dallas returned with the salesperson, and I told her the last item to add to the order.

"We have a delivery slot for five PM. It's our last one. Would you and your boyfriend be okay with that?"

"Oh, not..." I tried to correct her before Dallas freaked out, but I was the one getting ready to have a meltdown as he touched my lower back. Yet it wasn't just the touch. It was the slip of strong, slender fingers beneath my shirt that stroked along the skin above my waistband.

"Five is fine. How long will it take to move everything in?" Dallas asked.

"We send a three-person crew. It's not a large delivery since it's for an apartment. Maybe an hour and a half to two hours. Two people to move everything in and one person to assemble what needs done. Is that okay?"

"That's perfect," I answered. "We have to get a few things. Could you give us a call when the delivery people head out?" I stepped away from Dallas, a strange mixture of relief and loss at no longer having his fingers teasing the patch of hair on the small of my back.

"Of course." She smiled and turned. We followed her to the counter that she slipped behind and started tapping on the keys. "I already started the order, so the items are being gathered as we speak. I just have to add the last few pieces." I waited as she rang everything up, and I heard Dallas choke behind me as she told me the total.

Removing my wallet, I slipped out my credit card and handed it over. I wouldn't say anything, but I'd thought it would be more, especially with the same-day delivery. I would've paid extra just to get a bed delivered for that night or at least the couch.

"Is everything hooked up?" he asked.

"Yeah, they came in and installed the Wi-Fi the day after I moved in and mounted the TV above the mantle." I took the receipt and thanked her for all her help. We headed for the exit and stepped out onto the sidewalk. "There's a housewares place at the end of the block. We can get the basics to make it through the evening. Once everything's moved in, I'll know what to order."

"I think it's just outfitting the kitchen, pretty much."

"You're obsessed with the kitchen. Should I be worried? You're only in this for my kitchen." I teased him and tried to rein in my flirting. If I couldn't stop, maybe he'd just believe it was something I did naturally.

"Yes, it's all about the kitchen," he admitted as we walked down the block.

"You're killing my ego."

"I think it'll survive."

"You seem more...relaxed."

"This is Cusp of Summer Dallas, Fall, Winter, and Spring Dallas, completely different creatures."

"A few months of downtime is better than none."

"Thanks," he said as we stopped outside our destination.

"For what?" I asked as he opened the door for me and motioned me inside.

"For not telling me everything I'm doing is wrong." He grabbed a cart. "Yes, I know I spread myself way too fucking thin during the school year. I know things would be easier if I tried for a student loan, but do you know what a loan requires? Parents."

"They don't help at all?" I felt bad for him since I was financially able to pay for my son's tuition and books. Well, what his partial scholarship didn't cover. I paid his rent and bills, and he had a roommate, so it wasn't all that much. He was a good kid and never gave me any trouble. He was at the top of his class and hoping for medical school.

"Nope," he answered as we found the linen section. "They paid for my brothers, which is a kick in the balls, but they played the game, and I refused. I wouldn't give up my heathen friends. I didn't adhere to their abstinence-only teachings. There was a very awkward incident when I was sixteen with the Deacon's daughter." I looked at him and embarrassingly snorted at the look on his face.

"Your brothers are fucking your ex-girlfriend, though." I

grabbed what I needed in the way of sheets for both beds and moved to towels.

He shrugged his shoulders. "And maybe they know, but my brothers still did what our parents expected. There are rumors but no proof. She still plays the innocent when the situation calls for it. I tend to get into very awkward or embarrassing predicaments when I least expect it. What about you?" he asked as he grabbed a few glasses, mugs, and some silverware and put them in the cart.

"What about me, what?"

"You're finding out all about my shameful secrets, share. It'll make me feel better."

"I really don't have any."

"That's so boring. You're forty-two. You gotta have something, man."

"No, I was a good, clean-cut teenager. Played football. Never got in trouble. My parents always bragged to their friends."

"Until you came out? You don't have to answer if it's painful."

I shifted to wrap my hands around the top of the basket and looked at him standing on the other side. "My girlfriend was also in the closet. She came from a rich, upstanding family. When she got pregnant, we confessed to each other at the same time. So I thought telling my parents they were going to be grandparents would soften the blow of coming out. Afterward, Taria and I became the family we no longer had. Yeah, it hurt but not as much as pretending to be a person I wasn't. Taria and I would've done the right thing, gotten married, and lived together until we probably made each other miserable."

"I've met her a few times. I was moral support at the beginning when Carolyn was invited to the first few dinners." He paused. "But Taria found someone after the breakup," he said as we continued roaming through the store throwing things in the cart as we went.

"She did, very nice and sweet woman. I adore her. Taylor loves her. They met when she graduated from medical school. Leah's brother was in Taria's graduating class. She spotted her, and she fell head over heels at first sight."

"Sweet, one of those happily ever afters meant for those romance novels."

"I was happy for her. She brought her around after they were dating a few months to meet Taylor and me."

"If I overstep, tell me to shut up, but why did you become the full-time parent?"

"Taria was told she couldn't have kids. She had some female issues that started very early when she was around twelve, I think. So she'd never thought about having kids, she'd been told she could use a surrogate or adopt when she was older, but Taria, I think, disassociated herself from being a maternal figure. And when we found out, she went into a complete panic because women are forced into the role that one day they'd become wives and mothers. When she found out, she had a bit of a spiral because..." I didn't know how to explain it. Taria was a wonderful mother, just not one that was always present, but she never hid the fact she had a son.

"She felt like a shit human being?"

"Exactly. She was failing at what society claims is a fundamental function of being a woman. Men can just check out, not want to be the full-time parent, and it's just taken as normal. I was twenty-one and terrified, but I couldn't imagine not being a dad when his presence was just two lines on a test. I know because of the way I look, no one really got it."

"What's wrong with the way you look?" I glanced at him, and he appeared genuinely confused.

"I'm a big scary dude."

He snorted out a laugh, and I frowned. "My elderly grand-mother was scarier than you."

"Babe, really?"

He smirked at me. "Yes, really. You're not what is so-called socially fashionable or acceptable, so fucking what?"

"Thanks."

He rolled his eyes at me. "I'm a freckled, perpetually exhausted ginger. I'm adorable at best. Really not what a grown man likes to hear. Can you think of anything else we need before we check out? I think I'm finished with shopping and someone promised me dinner and a drink for helping today...on my day off, no less."

"No, I think everything is good for now. I'll give you my laptop, and you can outfit the kitchen." The way his honey brown eyes lit up made me feel good, soothed a bit of my ego that had been battered. Yet I was amazed at something so small making him happy. I'd bought expensive gifts, vacations, hell, the best of everything and had never earned that look before.

He was so fucking different from what I was used to. My world until a year ago was extremely superficial. Money, influ-ence, and the people you were fucking. I'd been so immersed in all of it that I didn't realize I'd missed certain things. Also, in some cases, discovered things I hadn't even known I'd taken for granted.

I wouldn't deny I craved the younger man, but I knew I couldn't have him. He wasn't attracted to me. He was my son's friend. If I made my intentions known, it would ruin every-thing, and I couldn't do that because I adored Dallas and the start of our friendship.

7
DALLAS

After my shift ended, I finally had a chance to check my phone and smiled at the messages from Lee. A lot of pictures and some grumpy pouting about all the deliveries he received and the boxes piling up in his apartment. He'd told me to get whatever I thought he needed. We'd sat on his new couch with his laptop, and not all those items were the ones I added to the cart.

I'd become uncomfortable when I saw the total amount and started to remove some things. He'd taken the laptop away and hit *confirm order*. I'd tried to get him to cancel some of them. While I knew he was well-off—he had enough to buy into a pub — but furnish and outfit an entire apartment without even blinking an eye? That wasn't me, though. I'd learned to be frugal. He just teased me as he ordered a small grocery delivery and our dinner.

"Why are you smiling at your phone?" Edwin, my boss, asked as he stood on the opposite side of the bar and finished up the deposit.

"A new friend. He asked me to help shop for his new place,

and let's just say he isn't happy with everything he now has to unpack."

I'd thought about going home, but instead, I'd stayed to hang out with my boss for a few minutes. Everyone was asleep, and I knew Lee started at the pub on the day shift the next day. Yet, I was tempted to go by his place. There was something about Lee that I liked more than I should.

For a man most people wouldn't want to meet in a dark alley, he seemed vulnerable. I sensed his ex-husband cheating on him had done a bit of emotional damage. When you're in a relationship with someone for a decade and a half, having it end in a betrayal probably made you insecure. Especially a marriage where you wanted to renegotiate the terms of keeping it open, and that request wasn't even considered, that had to hurt.

"Anything interesting about the new *friend*?" he asked and smirked at me.

"No, just friends. It's nice to not have every decision I make questioned. He just respects my choice."

"You're curious about said friend, though. I can tell."

I paused as I thought over what he'd said. Yes, I was curious, and while I wasn't bothered by that interest, I also didn't have any intention of breaking what we had. Yet it would be disrespectful to Lee to deny my attraction, and Edwin didn't know Lee, so I was safe to talk about the thoughts I'd been having. Not all thoughts. Some things I wouldn't share.

"Maybe, slightly curious."

"You really don't talk about your life outside this place. Which is weird because we know everything about everybody. I didn't know you were gay."

"I'm not." He arched a perfectly groomed brow, and I rolled my eyes as he set the paperwork aside. "I'm not. I've dated or hooked up with women. That's it. Be kinda weird if I suddenly found some man attractive."

"Why?" He paused, but I knew he wasn't waiting for me to answer. "Sexuality is ever-changing. I thought I was gay because I'd only ever dated men, but I grew up with same-sex parents in a progressive community for the time, and then I met my wife and realized I was bisexual or pansexual. My wife is a bi-demisexual. So you never noticing a man before doesn't mean the interest wasn't there, and you just overlooked it."

"He's my friend's dad," I confessed.

"Didn't take you for the older man type."

"I didn't take myself for the man type. I enjoy our friend-ship. I feel so much less stressed when I'm with him. Part of me wonders if the way he just grounds me has made me...I don't know. I'm confused."

"And you're always stressed and exhausted, honey. I'm not saying hop into bed with some man because you suddenly think you have feelings and you want to take a test drive. All I want you to do is think about it. When you're spending time with him, analyze what you like about him. If you just enjoy his pres-ence or if you imagine there could be a physical relationship."

I respected Edwin. He was a great boss, and he cared about the people who worked for him. Not to say he couldn't put his foot down, but as long as we did our job, we were really kind of a strange family. I didn't really have anyone other than Carolyn to ask for advice, but since he knew what I was going through, he told me his door was always open. "Thanks, I can't really talk about this with Carolyn."

"Why? She wouldn't judge you."

"That's not why. The man in question is her boyfriend's dad." I didn't appreciate his grimace.

"If complicated needed an example."

"You're not funny, boss man."

He chuckled. "My only advice for you is, don't take the possibility that you're romantically interested off the table. Spend time with him, enjoy a person who makes you relax. When did you meet him?"

"That week I took off." He nodded. "We went to the lake house that belongs to Taylor's dad. I got there early and said dad didn't know he was having guests. Let's just say I got more of a view than I was anticipating."

"Damn, that good? Lust at a glance?"

"No. I spun so fast I nearly made myself dizzy." But what I'd seen had been on my mind, though. Not just the thick hair that covered his body, but the length of his average dick. His bush at the base was just as abundant as the rest of his body hair. Strange things popped into my head, wondering if the hair was soft or coarse, what he'd smell like if I buried my face against his neck or chest, his pubes.

"I hope you don't look like that when you're with him. You're going to give yourself away." He laughed at me, and I huffed at him.

"Since you're going to be mean to me, I'm going home."

"You sure? I can drive you to your place. It's on my way home."

"No, I'll be fine. If I need to, I'll order a car. I might call him to talk to on my way home."

"Do that. I worry about you walking so late."

"I'll be good, promise. It's still early enough the bars are still packed."

He leaned across the bar, and I offered my cheek. I hopped off the stool and grabbed my backpack. As I exited the front, I slipped the straps of my pack up my arms and over my shoulders. I pulled out my phone and connected a call to Lee, maybe I should put some distance between us, but I didn't have to be led by my hormones.

"I have never had so much stuff." His deep voice was all guttural, and I laughed at his lack of a polite greeting.

"But you needed all that stuff," I assured him.

"I'll take your word for it. Why are you so late leaving work? It's almost one."

"I stayed back to hang out with my boss while he finished up the deposit."

"Are you walking?"

"Yes."

"Babe." I'd never been one for endearments, but from him, I didn't mind.

"I'm fine. I called you to keep me company on the long, lonely walk."

"I'll come get you."

"I'm fine, Lee. Excited about your first day?" I frowned as I heard him sigh. "What's wrong?"

"Nothing. I don't know. Before you ask, no, I'm not regretting the investment, but it's like starting from square one again. It just hit me."

I was concerned by his tone. "Do you want me to come over?"

"No, you need to go home to your bed."

Suddenly I preferred to be on his couch and maybe not have the expanse of a cushion between us as we stayed to opposite ends. Maybe find out what his lips left like. I mentally cursed myself and brought my thoughts back to where they needed to be—making Lee feel better. "Then don't bullshit me and tell me what's wrong. Don't do that uncommunicative masculinity shit with me."

"I'm a single man again. The business I worked my ass off to turn around is no longer mine. I'm starting at the bottom with employees who don't know me. I have to do this whole rebuilding trust again. I didn't anticipate that, at my age, I'd have to start over. My marriage wasn't perfect, but until that one incident, I could say I was happy or thought I was. And, yes, I know I agreed to an open marriage, but he broke our agreement, and all I can think is how many times he'd broken it before."

I didn't like how he sounded. I was used to his snark and wit, his naturally flirtatious personality. Something in me wanted to comfort him, but I knew that wasn't my place. "Then tell me what would make you happy? Say whatever. I won't judge."

"That's the thing, I don't fucking know. The finalizing of my divorce that made me officially single again, and then buying half a pub and creating a new home. I think it's all just getting to me."

"Which is normal, or I think it is. You're talking to someone whose relationships have mainly lasted until amazing mutual orgasms are achieved, and we part ways."

"I miss orgasms."

An inappropriate reply formed that I was more than capable of helping him with that, but I bit it back. "You know, at your age, I shouldn't have to inform you that orgasms don't need a witness." I grinned as he loudly laughed.

"You're extra snarky tonight. From the slightly awkward man to this incarnation, kind of shocking."

"I'm an introvert unless I'm in my spaces with people I like, and then watch out. You're just incredibly lucky that I'm comfortable with you."

"I really am, Dallas. Our friendship just started, but I value it...you don't know how much."

"Good, because you're stuck with me, my best friend kinda loves your kid. You sure you don't want me to come over, baby?

Seeing me will make you feel all better." I cursed myself at what I'd said and how it must've sounded.

All I could hear on the other end was his soft, steady breaths, and I wondered what was going on in his head. The silence lengthened, and it was strangely comforting, so I just waited a bit to let him process whatever he was thinking about. I thought about my own dilemma. Intellectually, I understood my attraction to Lee came out of nowhere. Yet I found myself helpless to ignore what every other part of me except my brain needed. Shouldn't I be more concerned about whatever I felt for him? Everything just slipped into place when I spent time with him—it was discovering that belonging I'd always searched for. Finally, finding where I fit a too addictive lure, and simply because it was with a man wasn't enough to ignore my growing attachment.

"Did you fall asleep on me?" I asked as I crossed the street to the block where my building was.

"N-no. I was thinking about you coming over, but I'm headed to bed, and you have to get in your own. You have to get all the sleep you can."

I groaned. "Don't remind me. I keep telling myself one more school year and it's all over, and I can get on with my life. Work a job I love. Maybe find someone to come home to."

"Is that what you want?" he asked softly, almost too quietly for me to hear.

"Yeah, why not? I'm not your typical twenty-two-year-old. I'm boring as fuck if you haven't noticed. The only reason I've stayed single is I don't think it would be fair to a partner to deal with my schedule."

"If they cared, they wouldn't be resentful of your ambition."

I wanted to demand to know if he'd feel neglected if he were mine, but I bit it back. As much as I was ready to be all-in, I sensed it would be too much for Lee to accept. "But people my age, not a lot of them would..." I took a deep breath as I tried to come up with a way to explain. "Compromise and honesty, they're important to me. I want someone who's all-in."

"As they should be. Okay, are you almost home?"

"I can see the front of my building. Trying to get rid of me?"

"No." His answer was short, and I felt my brows draw together. "No, I just want you to get enough sleep. I respect you, but that doesn't negate the fact I think you need more downtime."

"And I appreciate it." And I did. I liked that he cared. "I'm walking in now. As much as I want to keep talking, you need your rest, too."

"I do. Thanks for calling."

"You're welcome. Goodnight, and make sure you call or text me how your first day went, okay?"

"I will. Night."

I reluctantly disconnected the call and pushed the up button for the elevator. I should've told him I wasn't home just to keep our conversation going. The trip up to my floor seemed to take forever, and I pulled out my keys as I stepped out of the elevator. A few bulbs started to flicker as I made the long walk to my place at the end of the hallway. Unlocking my door, I entered and closed it behind me.

With a shake of my head, I took in my friends tangled on the couch. I turned away, walked to my room, and locked the door behind me. Envy burned in my chest. I'd never had someone to cuddle with. I'd imagined all kinds of things about when I was ready to find someone. I wanted someone I could love on, be affectionate with but would also submit to a hard fuck. Sexually, I embraced a dominance I didn't possess in my regular life.

I stripped out of my uniform, since it was one of my bar nights. I tossed my clothes into my overflowing hamper. That was a project for my next day off. I circled my bed to open my nightstand and removed my bottle of lube. Stretching out naked on my bed. I squeezed a small amount of slick in my left hand and hissed as the cool fluid coated my cock as I stroked the thick length.

My dick quickly hardened as I jacked my length and pictured a certain man straddling my hips. My image of Lee looked just right. His big furry body arched above mine as he spread his hands across my abs. His horseshoe mustache framed his curved lips. His teeth sunk into the bottom one as he bounced his burly body.

I wanted to know what his lips felt like. Did he growl or whimper when he got his ass pounded? Did he like to be fucked and taken however his partner wanted to use him?

I jerked off as I pictured everything, the wet head of his cock leaving pre-cum on my belly as the length slapped my skin. Him leaning forward to brace his hands above my shoulders as he rode me. I swore I could hear him. Smell his sweat. Feel the way his body hair felt sliding through my fingers, teasing the hollows between them.

My jaw clenched as I brutally fucked my fist as I sucked my stomach in. Goosebumps broke out on my smooth skin at the fantasy of him playing out. Fuck, I stroked faster as the contrast of my smooth body against his hairier one turned me on more.

I bit off a groan as my balls ached and my release hit me hard and fast, cum covering my hand as I worked my cock, jerking as I teased the head until I couldn't bear the touch. I laid there covered in sweat and my release, nowhere near satisfied, but I'd have to be. Yet how long would jerking off to fantasies of Lee be enough?

8
LEE

Like the pathetic man I was, my schedule had changed to match Dallas's, and I couldn't go to bed until I got a call from him or a text to let me know he was home safely. We hadn't seen much of each other in the previous weeks. We'd get together at the coffee place where we met the day we'd gone shopping before he'd head to work. Every time he arrived, I couldn't help but wonder what the younger man saw in spending time with me. I'd promised myself I'd tell him I was busy the next time he called or texted me, but I still agreed to show up.

Even though we were catching up for quick lunches or talking over a coffee, our time was still limited. I adjusted to my new normal, and he worked more hours to cover co-workers. A summer cold was moving through the city. I leaned back against the wall at the farthest end of the bar from the entrance and watched my friend bullshitting with some regulars.

I nursed my pint and kept checking my phone, we were still two hours from last call, and since Dallas was working, I hadn't felt like staying at home. Even for a slow night, Wednesday was still busy, and I felt more confident about my decision. I grinned at Tom as he told the customers bye and walked toward me. He spread his hands on the bar and kept staring at me, but I arched a brow as I remained silent. I'd known the man for nearly two decades. He'd worked security at the club with me until he'd quit to open the pub.

We'd become friends, but we hadn't spent a ton of time together in the last decade. Him and Roger hadn't liked each other at all, and Tom had made no secret about that. I waited him out, but the longer I didn't speak, the more his eyes narrowed.

"Cut the shit. Why are you stalking your damn phone? Who is he? Please tell me you're not reconciling."

I barked out a laugh at the horror on his face, and I should've fucked with him just for my own twisted amusement, but even I couldn't do that. As much of my life as I spent with Roger, I hadn't thought about giving it another go. In a moment of reflection, I'd come to the conclusion that what I'd had with my ex-husband no longer worked for me.

"A friend of mine gets off work between midnight and one, and he calls or texts me on his way home. He walks."

"A friend with benefits or something else?"

What did I want to admit to? I wasn't doing anything wrong being friends with Dallas, but I knew what people would assume. Hell, I lived for his phone calls and his texts, even the brief moments we hung out. His smile when he looked at me, and the way I felt like his full focus was on me. All of it was addictive.

"Something else, but not what you're thinking. He's just a friend. We've been hanging out and talking for about two months."

"What's he like?" he asked.

"Smart. Ambitious. Witty and snarky, and gorgeous, and twenty years younger than me."

His bushy eyebrows shot upward, and his shock was obvious. "You don't date or fuck younger men."

"No, I don't."

All my friends knew what my type was. Never been a secret that I typically fucked men like me. While a lot of men I knew were going younger with their lovers as they aged, I didn't have some point to prove. I glanced once more at my phone and saw no messages, and I frowned. He always responded when he turned his phone on.

"What's wrong?"

"It's twelve-thirty. He always messages me when he turns his phone on. He hasn't yet, and they close at..." A familiar tangle of ginger waves caught my attention as he broke through the small crowd. Damn, his t-shirt clung to his lean upper body, showed off the slight roundness of his pecs and his flat belly, and a pale strip of skin showed between the hem of his shirt and the waistband of his jeans. A hint of the treasure trail on display. I shouldn't even be allowed to be in the same room as that gorgeous man.

"Hey, baby, miss me?" he asked as he reached me, and I didn't miss Tom's gaze as it darted back and forth between us.

"You didn't text." I glared at him.

"Sorry, we all wanted out of there. A nightmare twenty-top table came in, and they were obnoxiously pretentious. We got all the side work and deposits done half-hour before official close."

"Poor baby, want a pint?"

"Yes, please, I'm off so I don't have to rush home." He leaned into my side. "You didn't answer if you missed me or not. I'm not feeling the love, Lee."

He was warm, and while he was lean, his body was strong. I wanted to twine my arm around his waist and pull him close. Maybe kiss that smug smirk off his fucking mouth. Find out how well his ass filled my hands, but that brought up visions of squeezing his ass cheeks as he was buried balls deep.

"Quit pouting. Before my friend jumps out of his skin, Dallas, meet Tom, Tom, meet my friend, Dallas."

"I've heard a lot about you recently." Dallas stretched his arm across the bar. They shook, and Tom still hadn't said a word.

"Fuck, you're beautiful," Tom muttered the compliment almost like a curse, and Dallas snorted.

"Thanks. I always welcome a stroke to the old ego. Lee is slacking."

Tom physically shook himself and turned away to pull Dallas a pint. Something burned in my belly and made my fists clench where I had them rested on my thighs. With shock and a little disgust, I realized I was jealous. Tom was a big burly guy like me, but he had those handsome looks that nobody could resist. I was in some weird limbo of middle-aged and still not looking like I'd reached forty-two yet. Classically or convention-ally handsome wasn't a descriptor anyone would use for me in my lifetime.

"Could you keep an eye on my bag and point me in the direction of the bathroom?"

I took his backpack and pointed through the crowd to the back hallway. He walked away, and I took deep, calming breaths. Over four decades of never experiencing a single second of that sickening feeling in my gut, I could do without it. The emotion made me want to tell Tom to back off, that Dallas was mine. Yet I felt stupid because Tom was a happily married man, him and his husband were obsessed with each other.

"Shit, man, warn somebody." Tom set the pint glass next to mine and glared at me.

"What did I do? I told you he was gorgeous."

"You didn't say he was a perfect specimen. I'm going to have to apologize to my husband now."

I snorted. "You can let Loren ogle someone to make amends."

"How have you not tried to get him into bed yet?"

"Because I don't want to fuck him." Which was true. I didn't. He was more important than that. Also, I was dying to be on the receiving end of being brutally railed by Dallas. My toy collection had several new additions since meeting him. Yet they were a poor substitute for what I fantasized the real thing would be like.

He shook his head at me, and I saw he was about to open his mouth but stopped as he glanced over my shoulder. I turned to find Dallas making his way through the crowd, and you couldn't miss the attention he received from most of the people in the room. Even if I wanted to ask him out despite him being straight and me taking a huge chance, there was no way I could compete with a lot better options than me.

Yet he didn't even seem to notice the looks he was getting. He just returned to me, slipped onto the stool beside mine, then grabbed his bag to drape one of the straps over his knee.

"How much for the pint? I'm just going to have one or two. I only came by because I knew Lee was here."

"On the house, you're friends with one of the bosses," Tom said. "He mentioned a friend of his was just getting off work."

"Yeah." Dallas mentioned the name of the restaurant, and Tom whistled through his teeth. "It's a nice place. I've been there for a little over three years. I found the job right before my freshman year. I like it. My boss is great because he works with students' schedules. Unfortunately, they're passing around a cold at work, so the last few weeks, Lee's been deprived of my attention."

I was studying Tom and then Dallas, and back and forth. Tom was enamored by Dallas. Dallas could have anyone eating out of the palm of his fucking hand, but he didn't realize it. While Roger liked to use his looks to his advantage, the thought would never even cross the young man's mind.

He had a bit of scruff on his cheeks. I couldn't resist as I raised my hand and stroked my curled fingers over his cheek. "Baby fuzz."

"Hey, that's two weeks of hard work by my follicles. Don't beard-shame me."

Tom chuckled, but I couldn't take my attention away from Dallas. His brown eyes were locked on mine, and there was that single-minded attention I got when we were together. How long had it been since I was someone's focus? I don't even think my ex-husband had ever done that with me.

"I'm sorry, babe." I forced my mouth into a flirty smirk to hide the way he affected me and brought my hands to my half-full pint. My brain and body screamed for me to touch him again, but I couldn't fucking do that. I'd already started to dangerously play with the fire that was my attraction to Dallas.

"No, you're not. You're smirking, and to think I was going to let you take me home with you."

My cock jerked, and I forced myself not to shift on the stool. I knew he only meant he was coming to hang out, but the way that sounded...I wanted it to mean so much more.

"You're still going to let me," I said as he rolled his big brown eyes.

"Bastard," he muttered as he sipped at his pint.

I wanted to scoot the stool all the way over and tuck my face against his neck. When we weren't together, I talked a big fucking game. I told myself that I was stronger than my urges, but if it was just my need to get off, that would be one thing. No, I wanted everything, and that terrified me. I wanted to submit, something no one else had ever let me do. Who would've thought the big bruiser wanted to drop to their knees and worship the beautiful man? I wanted Dallas to fucking own me.

9
DALLAS

We'd arrived at Lee's place at almost two AM, had a few beers on either end of the couch, and I'd watched him as his eyes grew heavy. I'd taken his bottle and placed it on the coffee table. He'd whispered thanks, and I hadn't taken my attention from him once as he drifted off. He shifted to stretch out his burly frame until his head rested on my thigh. I traced the edges of his sideburn and mustache, stroking my thumb along his lower lip. Even as I told myself no, I drew my fingertips down the front of his neck and slipped under his shirt. I groaned as I tangled my fingers in the springy curls on his chest. He whimpered in his sleep as I stroked my nails over his pebbled nipple.

Fuck, he was gorgeous and sweet, and so needy. As our friendship spanned into weeks and then months, I'd studied everything about Lee. For all his commanding presence, he submitted easily to my suggestions. I adored the way he turned shy and his thick, blond lashes would lower in an attempt to hide from me. In my gut, I knew no one had ever given him what I could—what I wanted to. He turned to bury his face against my stomach and nuzzled his cheek against my denim-covered dick. I shifted until I could turn sideways and worked myself down until I stretched out with him half-covering me, straddling my thigh and rutting his cock against me.

He felt so right and perfect, but I was still unsure of how to proceed. I knew about one-night-stands and sometimes anonymous fucks I picked up in bars or clubs. Everything in me required I claim him, I wouldn't settle for anything less, and the profound depth of that urge shocked me. Nothing in my life had prepared me for Lee. I accepted lust, I was fucking human, but with him, it was so much more. That *more* was what scared me the most. Not because I wouldn't jump at the chance. No. I worried about if he'd accept what I wanted him to be for me.

Selfishness made me take that moment with him for myself. Part of me knew that if he was awake, he'd keep a physical distance between us. I held him close with my right arm as he tucked his head under my chin. His hair was silky where it teased my skin. He fit so perfectly against me. I wanted the right to wake him up and lead him to the bedroom. I craved to keep him all to myself. My left hand stroked up his bicep and under his sleeve until I could tease my fingers and palm with the thick fuzz on his upper back. I'd never considered myself a tactile person, but I loved every second of the freedom to touch him.

He was so relaxed in my arms. I wondered when the last time someone had held him. Not in a sexual way but just to feel him. At the age of twenty-two, I learned I was obsessed with the older man and his happiness. He seemed so shocked when I focused on him, but I knew when I made my intentions known, he'd fight it. Whether he'd try to deny me because of my age or my friendship with Taylor. Neither of those things mattered to me, but maybe they meant a lot to him especially being out of a long-term relationship.

The last thing I remembered before closing my eyes was brushing a kiss to his forehead as I watched him sleep, and then

I'd awakened to find him in the same spot, but he had pushed my shirt up. His head was resting on my chest, and his right arm was hugging my waist so tight as if he were afraid I'd move away. I had no intention of doing that. In our time being physically apart, I'd dissected every emotion I had since I'd met him.

I'd never had the connection to a woman that I had with him. When I hooked up with someone, when we parted, I rarely thought about them or took advantage of a number if we even exchanged them. Every day he sent me texts to say hi, checking how my day was going, and I did the same for him. I knew he worried about me walking, and I called so he could hear my voice while I made my trip home because I knew it comforted him.

The fact I didn't know how to go forward frustrated me, so I decided we needed to spend more time together. Get him used to me being around. Touch him to build intimacy. He moaned, and I rubbed his back to soothe him to keep him asleep. Shit, the light on my phone flashed, and I stretched my arm to grab it. I unlocked it, and mentally cursed as I noticed several messages from Carolyn. Each one more frantic than the one before, I fisted my hand in his shirt and tugged the back up so I could get to skin and hair while I reluctantly connected a call to Carolyn.

She answered on the first ring screaming at me, and I had to pull the phone away from my ear.

"Good morning to you, too," I whispered but doubted it was going to keep my baby asleep.

"Where the fuck are you?"

"I crashed at a friend's place. We fell asleep watching a movie, but I swore I sent you a text to let you know I'd probably be home late or not at all. We had a few drinks."

"Why are you whispering? Are you safe?"

I chuckled and looked down as lips brushed my chest,

lightly sucked right next to my nipple, but he hadn't awakened. That was not the time for my cock to start perking up. He'd feel it against his belly. "We were asleep, and I'm trying to be quiet. We're going to have breakfast, and then I'll come home." I fingered the little rolls along his ribs, and he arched and moaned in protest as if it tickled.

"But you never spend the night."

"I was already tired. I shouldn't have had the four beers. Are you better now?"

"Yes, but double-check if you message me. When I saw your door open, I freaked out."

"I'm fine. What's going to happen when we don't live together anymore?" Shit, I bit back a groan as he licked slightly down my upper abdomen, and I felt guilty how much I wanted to urge him lower.

"When would that happen?"

I was confused for a second until I remembered the question I'd asked her. Thankfully, Lee paused his exploration before I did something impulsive like unzipping my jeans and feeding him the length of my cock. "What? When you get married, you're going to drag me along to live with you?"

"Of course." She sounded offended that I even asked.

I snorted too loudly and mouthed sorry as sleepy, blue eyes met mine. I held my breath, waiting for him to jump up, but something filled his gaze, an emotion I couldn't name, and then he was resting his head back on my chest.

"We'll have to discuss that later. Like I said, we're going to have breakfast, and then I'll be home."

It took a few more minutes to calm her down and ignore her questions about who I was with and where I'd met her. Carolyn and I never lied to each other, but this situation with Lee wasn't up for discussion yet. When I claimed him, it would be his decision on when we announced it, especially with my best friend dating my baby's son, and she told Taylor everything.

I disconnected the call. "Baby, I'm sorry, I didn't hit send on that text to Carolyn when we got home. She freaked out when I wasn't in bed. Did you sleep good?" I curled my fingers under his chin and tipped his head until he looked at me.

"Yeah, best sleep in a long time. You probably barely got a minute. You should've woken me up."

"No, I don't remember falling asleep. I only woke up a few minutes before I talked to Carolyn. I would've been quiet until you were ready to get up on your own. You looked too comfortable."

"I'm sorry," he whispered as he pulled my shirt down.

"It's fine. Nothing you could do would offend me. I think you just wanted warm skin. Probably too slick for you. You did beard-shame me last night." I winked at him, but I remembered the exact feel of his fingers. His stroke of my cheek the previous night had been a bit tentative, as if he were scared to upset me. My baby would be shocked at what I'd allow him to do.

He glared at me, and my stomach jumped as he stroked under the hem of my shirt. "You're perfect, and you know it. You had my friend who's completely obsessed with his husband blurt out you're beautiful. You're just fishing for compliments." He pushed up, and when he was straddling my hips, I grabbed his sides.

"What do you want for breakfast? I want to feed you before I leave." How many times had I imagined him in this position? I forced myself not to rub his hard dick against mine and delay feeding him.

"You'll have to see what I have. I'm going to hop in the shower and change. Do you want some sweats and a t-shirt so you can clean up before you go?"

I loved he wasn't in a hurry to move away. "No. I'll shower

when I get home." I squeezed his side. "Go get all pretty, and I'll have something made by the time you're done."

"Pretty? You're just being an ass."

I tightened my hands around his waist and kept him from moving. "When I say something to you, I mean it. Do you understand me?" I caught the way a hard swallow worked his throat and he was nodding, and I let him go. I laid there until I heard his feet on the stairs to the loft, and then I jumped up to take a piss and then get started on feeding my baby.

He didn't understand what he meant to me, but I also didn't think he was ready to hear it. Lee deserved some romance and seduction because I don't think he'd ever had that before. I knew I didn't have a way to spoil him with material things, but I was more than equipped to pamper him in other ways. I was tired of holding myself back.

10

LEE

I'd cursed myself for two days after waking up with Dallas, and when I should've made an apology and put space between us, I'd laid there listening to him on the phone. I couldn't believe I'd shoved his shirt up in the night to get to bare skin. And he'd seemed content to lie there and let me cuddle against him as if it were fucking normal. As I'd stared down his body, all I could think about was jerking his jeans open and sucking him off, the thick ridge of his cock against my ribs a cruel temptation. My mouth watered at the thought of him fucking my throat as he pulled at my hair.

A groan slipped free, and I dropped my forehead to my desk. Tom and I shared the office, and I was so glad I had it to myself for my breakdown. Him and his husband, Loren, were off on a date night. The door opened, but I didn't bother lifting my head. Hopefully, whoever entered just thought I was napping and not having some crisis. I was too old, too rough for all the bullshit I was putting myself through. All it would take was a phone call, and I could have several men ready to bend over for me, but I couldn't, and it sucked.

"You know, six months, and I had to find out from our son

where you were hiding," Taria's amused voice had me looking up. She was a gorgeous leggy blonde with supermodel potential and the personality of drunken, foul-mouthed biker. Since she'd started as an ER doctor, I think she'd gotten worse. I adored her.

"My phone works, and I have the same damn number."

"You were mourning the mediocre dick you've been sucking for fifteen years."

"It's always a pleasure." I glared at her until her beautiful face brightened with a massive smile.

"Also, our son is concerned, hence the rescue mission. Get your shit. Let's go get greasy food."

I frowned at her. "Why is Taylor concerned? He hasn't mentioned it, and we talked yesterday." I pushed up from my chair and walked around the desk. I kissed the cheek Taria offered me. One of the things I'd prided myself on being a dad was my son never hesitated to come to me. To find out he sent in reinforcements worried me.

We made our way to the front of the house, and I told Ally, the senior on-duty bartender, I was taking a dinner break with a friend and to call me if they needed anything. Taria still hadn't said a word by the time we exited into the humid evening.

"Are you going to explain?"

"Taylor just said you seemed to be having some issue adjusting to single life. He noticed you haven't been seeing any of your *friends*."

"Our son sent you to interrogate me because I'm not fucking anyone?"

"Exactly." She wrapped her arm around mine as I shoved my hands in my pockets. "Lee, you're an extremely sexual person, you enjoy the connection, and that hasn't changed since we started dating in high school. So the fact you went from regular husband dick and sometimes three benefit dicks a week for years to complete abstinence? It's kinda concerning, honey. So tell me what's going on?"

What was I going to say? I fell for a younger, straight man, and there I was, the hairy Bear who scared most people just by being suddenly feeling insecure. That I was in the middle of an identity crisis wasn't helping matters. I'd viewed myself a certain way my entire life, and to suddenly not know who I was fucked with me.

"Man, come on." She shook me.

"You know I tried to change the arrangement with Roger."

"Which he was a shit partner and didn't even allow the fucking discussion. I told you to leave the first time you told me he wouldn't even compromise on it."

"Other than you, I never did the whole monogamous bull-shit. I had my vices, I loved my vices, and him fucking other people never bothered me. And when he asked me to marry him, well, I didn't see a reason to change it. If it ain't broke and all that."

"The question is, why didn't it bother you? Listen, I'm all for sex positivity and not adhering to some heteronormative stan-dard of relationships, but there's a point when we evolve, and that bastard of an ex-husband...there was no evolution. He was still covered in primordial ooze disguised as hair gel and anti-wrinkle serum."

I snorted and shook my head. "At first, it was making up for lost time. I'd denied being gay for years, and it was fucking great to let loose. To have no shame in fucking a good-looking guy. I was in my twenties. What the fuck did I know?"

"True, but your hairy ursine gorgeousness was wasted on the knock-off *Ken* doll. I mean, seriously, man, no wonder you needed outside dick." She rubbed my forearm. "We don't spend enough time together."

I agreed. Before we'd even become a couple, we were best

friends and I'd loved her. "We don't, the past almost year and a half, with Roger breaking our agreement, selling my percentage of the club, finding a new place to live...buying into another place. It's just been fucking insane."

"Then tell me what's actually wrong, friend-code, just between you and me, and I'll tell our son that you're fine, just processing."

"I caught feelings."

"Like *feelings* feelings?"

"Yeah, as high school as that sounds." I chuckled as she pinched my love handle.

"Well, don't be an asshole, tell me."

"He's gorgeous." She groaned. "It's not just about his looks. He's ambitious and smart, a bit awkward until you get to know him, and then all bets are off. He's witty and fun, affectionate."

"Okay, I'm not seeing the issue here."

"He's twenty-two, and as far as I know, straight." I snorted as she violently shook me.

"We don't mess with the straighties. The Het crushes are a one-way street to a fiery inferno of a crash."

"The age doesn't bother you?"

"Nah, the age gap is only an issue with the persons with the gap. Where did you meet him?"

I just said fuck it. She enacted the friend-code, so I braced myself and confessed. "He's a friend of Taylor's."

"Holy shit, Lee, hit the brakes, man." She practically hissed at me.

"Well, he's Carolyn's best friend. I met him when they came up to the lake house." I frowned as she completely froze and spun until she was facing me. Her maniacal expression frightened me. It was the same one she shared with our son when they were onto some epic bullshit.

"Dallas. Ginger, too gorgeous for his own good, Dallas?" A

forty-two-year-old woman hysterically giggling was terrifying. "A man so beautiful he makes lesbians question themselves, Dallas?

"Shit." I groaned and should've known better.

"Oh, this was well worth the visit. Have you been spending time with him?"

"Um, yes." I was glad when we got back to walking because I didn't want to see her expression. I already sensed she was plotting. "A few weeks after I got back from the lake, we ran into each other one night after he got off work. I walked with him to a diner, and I gave him my number...just to have him text me when he got home. It was late."

"Uh-huh, please continue."

I rolled my eyes. "I told him if he ever had a night off, I'd buy him a drink and to text me. A week later, he did. He helped me shop for furniture. We spent most of the day and evening together."

"Has this gone beyond..." She paused.

"No, and it's not going to. We talk or exchange messages every day. We meet up for coffee. He came by the pub the other night when he got off work. We fell asleep on the couch. I woke up laying on him like a fuzzy, weighted blanket. I'm not equipped for this bullshit, Taria. To me, sex is sex. It doesn't need an emotional connection. That's proven by the fucking fact that me and my ex-husband fucked countless other people in our fifteen-year relationship. Dallas met Tom, and I got...jealous," I whispered the last word.

"Um, hold up, man, you don't have one jealous bone in your body."

"That's what has me freaking out. It's like an identity crisis. Not to mention the butch man before you is dying to get owned."

"You should go for it."

"What were you saying about staying away from the straighties?"

She waved off my question with a small smile. "People have the right to change their minds."

"I don't cuddle. I don't get soft over men. I definitely don't think about doing more than getting my dick slick and then moving on. Hell, I practically did that with Roger. What am I even playing at here?"

"You're not playing at shit. At the ripe old, mature age of forty-two, you met the one you don't want to share. It's a sign. You should feel it out. If nothing else, Dallas is super grounded for being twenty-two. Maybe you can have a few months of a dick attached to a man with model potential."

"I don't want to fuck him, Taria. That's the problem."

I moved us towards a diner where we'd both eaten before, and I opened the door for her. We walked in and automatically went to a corner booth in the farthest corner. Her and I had always been attuned, and I think that's why our relationship worked so well. We'd always known what the other needed or wanted. She slid onto the seat, and I sat opposite her as we reached for the menus in the metal table holder. I leaned to the side to pull my phone out and placed it on the table in case I was needed.

She kept studying me as the server arrived, we ordered drinks, and since we already knew what we wanted, burgers and fries, we went ahead and added those. Taria's silence was annoying me. She had this way of processing. It was the same with Taylor, so I just let her work out whatever was in her head. After our drinks arrived and we were left alone again, she grinned at me.

"What's going on? Just say it."

She softly laughed. "Nothing, I missed this. We spent almost five years together as a couple, a decade before those as best friends. Every day and night that we weren't working, it was always the two of us." I saw a familiar expression.

"Quit with the guilt and regret. It's not like you bailed. You got him weekends and holidays, or whenever he called to say he wanted to spend the night with you and Leah. So what if the male parent was the full-time one. You were there for all the important shit, school plays, graduations...you put in the time, Taria. Our family was just a little more unconventional, but we have a great kid despite whatever mistakes we think we made."

"True, and Leah and I both agreed Taylor was enough. She loves him like he was her own. Sometimes it just hits me with what-if."

"The what-if doesn't matter, we did what we did, and he turned out just fine."

"Yeah, you were the best option of a full-time parent anyway. You were way more maternal than I was, and even if we stayed together, could you imagine you with your club hours and me with medical school, then residency. We would've killed each other."

"Ha, ha, ha." My phone beeped, and I went to pick it up, but Taria got to it first. She put in my code because it never changed, and her face lit up. "What?"

"Dallas wants to see you. Wants to know if he can come to your place tonight after he gets off work. I don't think he's as straight as you think." She flipped the phone around for me to take it.

Dallas: *Can I come by after work? It's been a shit night, and I want to see you.*

Lee: *Sure. Are you okay?*

Dallas: *I am now. I'll let myself in. I got the door code and see you when you get home.*

Something bloomed almost too warm in the center of my chest and caused my stomach to flip. I made him feel better just by telling him he could come over. There was also the way he'd told me he'd see me when I got home. I felt odd about how that had affected me.

Lee: *Okay, I'm having a late lunch with Taria.*

Dallas: *Tell her hi if you're comfortable. I gotta get back out front.*

I locked my phone. "He said to tell you hi if I was comfortable. Do you think I gave him the impression something's wrong with us being friends?"

"Have either of you told Carolyn or Taylor you two have been hanging out?"

"No, but I've introduced him to my friends. I know he told Carolyn the other morning that he spent the night at a friend's place. He's not some dirty secret, Taria. I like having him all to myself."

"It'll be fine. It's not like you two are doing anything wrong. You're both consenting adults."

"Yeah," I agreed, but there was a sick feeling in my gut that I'd done this the wrong way.

"Let's just enjoy our food, and you can get back to work and then home to your beautiful man."

I shook my head and groaned. "And I really want him to be mine."

"I know you do. I can see it on your face. Even stressed about it, Dallas makes you happy, but don't let it go on to the point that happiness turns to misery when you ignore you're falling in love with him." She grabbed my hand and squeezed as I nodded.

I was fucking falling for him. You didn't think about a man all day, every day, and pretend it was normal to feel that way about a friend. Yet I didn't know what to do, but I had to figure it out. Did I just go for it, or as Taria said, feel it out a bit? Maybe he wanted me, too.

11

DALLAS

My feet felt like they dragged as I walked down the hallway to Lee's apartment. He'd texted me to say he'd probably get out of there a bit early because the bartender said she'd cover him. I should've gone home, but I'd had a shit night. Everything that could go wrong had. It seemed as if none of the customers were happy with anything. A few waitresses had made the mistake of giving their numbers to a supposedly successful businessman, and he'd come in that night without knowing they were both working and had a date with him.

Men were fucking morons. Edwin had threatened to fire all of us at least once that night. The two servers had acted professionally until they got to the back of the house, but all bets were off then. We'd spent way too much time in the weeds, too. I'd had to change out of my kitchen uniform to my server dress shirt and apron to cover the tables while Edwin diffused the nuclear war.

And all I'd wanted was a few minutes with my baby. He made everything better. I keyed in the door code, turned the handle, and headed straight upstairs to his bedroom. I hoped he didn't mind if I borrowed a pair of sweats. I dropped my back-pack on the floor at the foot of his bed, toed off my non-slip shoes, and stripped off my shirt on the way to his bathroom.

I removed all my clothes and stretched my arms over my head, trying to work out the kinks from being tense all night. We rarely had employee meltdowns, but when it did happen, they were all pretty epic. I turned on the taps and moaned as the strong water pressure hit my skin. My shower at home was pathetic in comparison.

I washed off the film left over from the kitchen, washed my hair, and then tipped my head forward to let the water beat down on the back of my neck. The only thing that would make this better was if Lee was with me. But I'd have to settle for the scent of his body wash on my skin. If I was lucky, I'd get another night of sleeping with him pressed to my side.

Shit, that reminded me I had to let Carolyn know I wouldn't be home again, or she was going to have another freak-out. Days had passed, and she hadn't forgiven me for worrying her yet. Between the warmth and the massage of the water, I was getting far too relaxed. I turned off the shower, got out, and picked up a towel off the shelf next to the large stall. I dried off, found one of the extra toothbrushes Lee kept in a bottom drawer, and finished getting ready to relax.

After cleaning up the bathroom, I gathered up my clothes to shove them into my bag. I wasn't a neat freak, but I knew Lee liked to keep everything orderly with his odd schedule. I crossed the room to Lee's dresser and found a pair of well-worn, soft sweats. Dressed and ready, I took my phone to the living room and stretched out on the couch facing the door so I could see Lee as soon as he walked in. I hit the green button to connect a call to Carolyn. We were both night owls, so I knew she'd answer.

"Where the hell are you?"

"You're making that demand a lot lately."

"Well, you're being secretive as fuck, and usually you tell me everything."

"I won't be home tonight, probably just to come back in the morning and change for work."

"Who is she? It's the same one, right?"

"Yes, it's the same person, but I don't want to talk about it yet." I didn't feel completely comfortable not telling Carolyn. No way was I ashamed of the fact I wanted a chance with Lee. We had to work out a few things, and I didn't want to expose myself until I knew if he wanted a relationship. If it all imploded, at least I wouldn't have to avoid all the *are you okay* inquiries.

"Why? What's the big deal?" I heard the hurt in her voice, and I grimaced because I loved her and hated that I couldn't share something I was excited about.

"We haven't talked about it, and I don't know if we're on the same page, but I want this one to work out."

"Sex that good?" she asked as she giggled.

I snorted at her question. "There's been no sex."

Her gasp was loud and obnoxious. "No sex and you're spending the night with this mystery person. You're in love."

I wouldn't deny that I adored the man, but until I knew what was happening between us, I didn't want to let my guard down too much.

"I won't deny that I adore them. It was a shit night at work, and I just"—I paused as the door opened—"wanted to see my friend. So if I can't use the washer and dryer here, I'll be home to grab clothes in the morning before work. I just didn't want you to worry."

"Your friend home? Because you're trying to get rid of me. Put me on speaker."

"Carolyn, I am *not* putting you on speaker. I'm not that

cruel." Her offended gasp made me chuckle. "And someone very sexy walked in so I'm getting off the phone."

She argued with me for a few minutes, and then I disconnected the call. I'd hear how rude I was the next day. I stretched out my arm to set my phone on the table, and then I really looked at him.

"You're looking a little worse for wear. Maybe I wasn't the only one with a rough night."

"Dude came in, thought the servers were on the menu. I stepped in, blocked a broken bottle but ended up with the contents on me as he smashed it. The cheap beer stench is too much. I'm going to take a quick shower and be right back. Find something for us to watch."

Once he left, I sat up, picked up the remote, and found some gory horror movie. At least we shared a love of horror. After I picked it, I didn't hit play but got up to go to the kitchen to grab a few bottles of water and sodas. Then it hit me that he may not have had dinner, and I went to find him. The shower was running, so I leaned into the bathroom.

I called his name, and the stall door clicked open, and he leaned out slightly. "Are you okay?"

I was too distracted by the way the water had slicked down the usual fuzziness of his chest, stomach, and arm hair. "Did you have dinner? I can make you something."

"I had a late lunch and then grabbed a sandwich before the kitchen closed down. I know it doesn't meet your standards."

"Well, at least you ate. Finish your shower. I picked a movie."

He stepped back into the stall, and the door clicked. I tipped my head back and wondered why the universe wanted to torture me like that. I returned to the kitchen, grabbed our drinks, and took my spot back on the couch, tossing the cushions over the back to make room. I was getting a damn cuddle in no matter if it was a mistake or not.

I closed my eyes while I waited, picturing my baby just upstairs, naked and wet. After I woke up with him, all I thought about was holding him again.

"Are you asleep?"

As I opened my eyes, I shook my head and hopefully hid my disappointment at him dressed in pajama bottoms and a v-neck t-shirt. I scooted all the way back and patted the spot in front of me. "Lay down. It'll cut out the middleman of you climbing on me in your sleep."

I thought he was going to refuse, but I noticed the way his gaze lingered on the spot, and then he was sitting down. As he leaned to the side, his head came to rest on my bicep, his back pressed to my chest, and the perfect muscled ass was cradled by my hips and thighs. I laid my arm over him and cupped the adorable curve of his belly.

"Hit play and just relax. We both had shit nights."

"What happened with yours?" he asked.

"Two servers gave their numbers to a customer. They both slept with him on separate occasions. He came in with a date while both were working. Nuclear meltdown. And it just seemed like nothing went right. It was like one thing went wrong, and it was just a clusterfuck of dominos falling." I nuzzled the crown of his head and took in the clean, masculine scent of his shampoo.

"This isn't weird for you?"

I didn't pretend not to know what he was asking me. "No, why would it be?" I asked as I flexed my arm to pull him closer to my chest, and I still wasn't satisfied.

"You're spooning a man."

"My masculinity isn't fragile. I don't think affection between men is some horrific thing. Besides, we've already done this once, and nothing bad happened. I just want you to decompress."

He nodded, and as the movie played, I memorized how perfectly he fit me. There was only an inch or two difference in our heights. Yes, he was broader, maybe had a good fifty pounds on me, but while he was strong and burly, he had this softness to him I loved. There wasn't anything I didn't adore about Lee.

That's why I'd needed to come to him. We made everything okay for each other. I understood what he needed; affection outside sex had been denied to him. He'd had a bastard of a husband who was a fool for not wanting to claim every part of Lee. It was incredulous that whoever belonged to Lee would want to touch anyone else.

I stroked his belly, to his side until I palmed his hip, and moved over his broad muscled thigh. The more I petted him, the quicker he relaxed until he started softly snoring, just deep rumbles. I smiled as he grabbed my right arm and hugged it to his chest. I wanted to be so good to him. Just a bit more patience, and then he was all mine.

12
LEE

I rubbed my bare chest right over the spot where Dallas had his hand fisted in the curls that morning when I woke up. His left arm had been under my shirt and curved around my stomach. In all my years, I'd never cuddled with a man. I'd been the big spoon for Taria a few times, and we'd shared the middle of our bed. But my hookups were never all-night affairs, and Roger just wasn't into physical affection outside sex, maybe a few quick hellos or goodbye kisses. He wasn't the demonstrative type, and it hadn't mattered so much back then, but a need grew to connect with someone on more than a sexual level.

Dallas had completely curled around me and had covered us with a blanket I'd folded over the arm of the couch sometime in the night. Even after my talk with Taria, I was still lost in a crisis. On the one hand, I'd always considered myself pretty self-aware, assuming I knew what I wanted. But on the other, all this crazy shit was filling my head. Like I'd told Taria, I believed we all required at least one vice, and I'd loved the supposed freedom.

Shit, I'd never considered what I'd wanted to start to creep in, though. *Monogamy*, I'd embraced a life where I didn't conform to some bullshit societal morality that said multiple partners were bad. Sex to me was about getting off. Who didn't want to feel good? Yet as I'd aged and maybe matured from recently out gay man to an older one, I think I'd wanted to see what it was like to have a man who treated me as his sole focus.

Then there were the insecurities of getting older. Your body no longer toned, and shit started heading south. The rules on what was trendy in all the magazines and on TV. Fuck, I hated those arbitrary rules that were dictated and were expected to follow. Just bullshit to make you a carbon copy of everyone else. Why the fuck did I need to wax or shave—lose weight for perfect sculpted abs? Even back in the day, I'd always had a layer of insulation.

I wouldn't deny I'd had a bout of internalized homophobia and toxic masculinity from growing up and my time denying who I was. Life in the closet wasn't the way to be good to your-self. I'd worked on it, I couldn't do much for the outside, but I'd dropped most of the fucked-up behaviors I'd learned from making my sham heterosexuality above reproach. A lot of that bullshit had followed me into my relationship with Roger.

The door opening pulled me from my spiraling thoughts, and I felt like a bit of an ass when I was disappointed not to see Dallas coming in.

"Hey, Dad." Taylor kicked off his shoes and dropped his backpack. It was like a flashback to when he'd come home from school.

"Hey, honey. What are you doing here?"

"I sent you a few texts that I had some time to kill and was visiting. You're gonna make me insecure with your lack of enthusiasm at seeing your only child." He padded over to the couch and fell next to me to press against my side.

"Knock it off," I said as I picked up my phone to see a few texts, but I wouldn't have any from Dallas until later. He normally didn't turn on his phone until his shift was over. "And did you need to sic your mother on me?"

He choked out a laugh. "I called in the big guns."

"I told you at the lake house, I'm fine."

"I know, but you've always been the upbeat parent. A little gruff, but...you're not dead."

"Thank you for confirming that." I rolled my eyes at him, and he elbowed me. I playfully grunted as if he'd wounded me.

"All I'm saying is, starting to date again wouldn't be a bad thing."

"Taylor, I love you, I do, but I had this arrangement with Roger. It was simple, just be honest with me if you're fucking someone else. I always trusted him, he had permission to date or hook-up with anyone he wanted, but the rule was to let me know. He lied about one man. How many others had he lied about? That fucked up my trust and my sense of safety that he was being responsible. Just saying something is okay doesn't mean you're okay."

"I get that. I do, Dad. And Pop was a major dick for what he did, but just one teeny, tiny, little date." He held up his right hand with the tips of his thumb and index finger almost touching.

"I've actually been thinking about it."

"Yes," he shouted, and his excitement made me chuckle. My son had always made me happy from the first second I'd held him in my arms.

Yet, I wondered if his excitement would withstand the fact that the person I wanted was a friend of his. I didn't want to hurt his friendship with Dallas. My son loved Carolyn. Would it put stress on their relationship? There were so many what-ifs, and I fucking hated not knowing what I wanted to do. When I made a decision, I always went for it—no fear or second thoughts. This new insecurity was killing my confidence.

"Does this person have a name?"

"Yes, but I don't think we're at the point where I'm going to share it with you."

"Man, why?" he whined and turned to set his chin on my shoulder, batting his lashes. "Are you ashamed of me? The product of your *confused period*?" He air quoted when he said confused period.

"I wasn't confused, I knew, and if I could've convinced myself I was bi, I'd probably still be with your mother. My love for her wasn't confusion." A lot of people hadn't gotten that when I said I'd been happy with her and that I'd loved her, but I refused to apologize for loving someone, especially Taria. She'd had my back and I hers for most of our lives.

"I know. You two were amazing. I got lucky. I've seen the cluster that was some of my friends' relationships with their parents. Can you at least tell me if the guy is nice?"

"He's extremely nice, intelligent, and ambitious, not flakey. He's affectionate. That's taking some getting used to."

"At least tell me he's not a Roger two-point-oh."

"He's not, not in any way. I'm just unsure if I want to do more than be friends with him. I like him a lot. And I worry if I put a sexual component in the mix that it'll ruin things." Which was true enough. Dallas's affection confused me the most. It wasn't even all about his emotional maturity at an age where I'd only thought with my dick. I knew the theory no one was mentally or emotionally mature enough until their thirties to know what the fuck they wanted, but he was so confident I rarely thought about our age difference.

"Just as long as you're trying, you're too young to shut down because you have an asshole ex."

I was about to answer when my phone beeped. I grabbed it from where I'd placed it on the couch beside me.

Dallas: *You home?*

I started to type out yes and ask when he'd be there, but instead, I panicked.

Lee: *Taylor is here.*

Dallas: *Oh, okay, I'll see you tomorrow then.*

I sensed his disappointment, and I felt like an ass. Was I doing what I'd feared? Keeping him secret and hurting him in the process to keep him all to myself. Why couldn't I just be honest that I'd made friends with Dallas after meeting him? I frowned as minutes went by without a response.

"What's wrong?"

"Nothing, everything's good." I checked my notifications one more time and still didn't have a reply. Maybe I really was an asshole. I'd make up for that, but first, I had to figure out how.

"Is that the mystery man? I can leave."

"No. He's probably busy. He just wanted to say hi." I'd gotten used to our nights of movies and him making me dinner, talking about anything and everything. I think he knew more about me than anyone else.

"That's not what your face says."

"It's fine, now catch me up." I put my arm around him in our *we're going to talk* position, and he turned to lean against my side. I brushed my lips to his soft blond hair.

"Carolyn is freaking out."

"What's wrong?" Carolyn could be a little high-strung, but she was one of these naturally bubbly people who had never met a stranger. She was assertive and fearless. Those were the first things I'd noticed and loved about her.

"Dallas has been being a bit weird. and she's worried he's starting to burn out."

I was already grimacing about the partial lie I was about to tell. "Well, from what I remember, he puts a lot of pressure on himself."

"Yeah, and we get that, but this is a man who was a home-body. If he's not at work or school, he's at home. Suddenly, he's spending the night at some mystery woman's place. Coming home some mornings or afternoons just to change and get to work. But he won't say anything...no details about the person. We're happy he met someone."

"Then why are you worried about it?"

"Okay, don't get me wrong, Dallas is a great guy, but I mean, he's a middle-aged man in a twenty-two-year-old body. He's so focused on work and school. All he cares about is getting his life and career started. I've known him for over a year since Carolyn and I started dating, and even I've noticed a difference." He paused and seemed to take a breath. I was getting worried, and I saw him all the time if we weren't busy. "He's attached to his phone. He's smiling over text messages, for fuck's sake. He never does repeats, and I was traumatized by the one time I walked in when he had a girl over. There are some things that you don't expect to hear from someone as mild-mannered and awkward as Dallas. He has a PhD in dirty talk, and there are some friends you don't need to know their kinks."

I froze but snorted out a laugh at the same time. There were things I didn't need to know. I already had enough of an issue, but to be honest, it was always the quiet ones that would shock you. "Such a prude."

"I'm not a prude. I was raised by you and Mom. There's no room for shame. But the thing is, Carolyn said there's been no sex, and he's spending nights. He says he really likes the person, and we're happy, but it's just like a complete turnaround the last four months."

Damn, had I already been hanging out with Dallas for four months? We'd met late March, and it was Mid-July. It didn't seem like that long. And my brain dangerously latched onto Dallas saying that he really liked the mystery person, like I was a teenager finding out my crush liked me. Another element to add to my already long list of items pertaining to my identity crisis. "If he's happy, then what's the issue?"

"The secrecy. He tells Carolyn everything, and it's kinda hurt her feelings. I think something was mentioned about him not knowing if they wanted to make things public." He shrugged. "She's just worried he's going to get his heart broken because this is the first person he's mentioned that hasn't been like a one-night stand, and he rarely mentions those. She just notices by how often condoms get added to the shopping list on the fridge. And let me tell you, for a person who doesn't get out a lot, he's extremely active."

My chest tightened, I'd tried to ignore that he was a gorgeous, sexually active man, but did he hook up on the nights we couldn't get together? Was that where he would end up tonight since I'd told him Taylor was there? That flash of jealousy was back, and I was a bastard for being mad that my friend wasn't in my bed. I was hating these feelings bullshit; I was going to get hurt, and I could already see it was coming.

"Let him have his fun. I know Carolyn worries, and I understand it, but isn't she happy he's taking something for himself that has nothing to do with working and school?"

"She is." He glanced at me. "We're both happy. We've been telling him forever to relax, but one minute he has this single-minded focus on graduating and working to cover his tuition to this mystery person."

"I know, but let him say something when it's time. He seems like a level-headed guy, and as we all know, sometimes sex for people is a great stress-relief."

"True, but it's just hard because I can't seem to make my girl feel better, and I feel kinda helpless. The only thing I could do is confront Dallas to let him know what's going on with her."

"You're a great partner to Carolyn. You'll do what you need

to do, but you can't make someone talk when they aren't ready."

"True."

"You want to stay for dinner? I worked the day shift and did all the paperwork this morning, so I don't have any plans."

"Sure, Carolyn has a friend from work who just got engaged. They were all going out to celebrate. Do you think twenty is too young to know what you want?"

"Something you want to tell me?"

"Not that, Dad." He chuckled. "I love her, I really do. Right now, I could say she's the one, but she's twenty-one and graduating next year, and I've got another two years and then medical school."

"You're a great match. I like her and think she's good for you. You do what feels right for you, and you know, your mother and I will support you however you need. You know Taria fell in love at first sight with Leah. Maybe it's genetic."

I gave him a squeeze as I picked up my phone and frowned at still not having a notification from Dallas. Shaking my head, I pulled up the delivery app and handed the phone to Taylor for him to choose. I internally stressed about how to make up to Dallas for probably making him feel unwelcome. I'd call him later after Taylor went home and smooth things over and maybe figure out how to tell my son that I'd secretly been hanging out with one of his best friends for months.

13
DALLAS

August had arrived and brought miserable temperatures, and that sometimes made working in a kitchen worse. I'd also started spending all my time with Lee. On the nights he worked, I let myself in and took a shower, and I stretched out on the couch to wait for him to get home. It was one of our rare days where we were both off early. I punched in the code for his door lock and turned the handle, balancing a large cup and a to-go bag.

I'd made my baby a special late lunch, and later, I was taking him out for a movie and dinner. Although, the incident a few weeks earlier was bothering me. I'd texted him like always, but he'd said Taylor was at his place. He'd warned me away, and that hurt, but I wasn't much better since I wasn't sharing with Carolyn about my ongoing romantic seduction of Lee.

"Hey, baby, you home?" I called out as I closed the door and froze at finding him shirtless in his kitchen. His pajama bottoms hung low on his hips. Fuck, it was getting harder not to touch him and that he tended to fall asleep and seek me out for a cuddle made my patience grow thinner.

"How was work?" he asked as he turned around.

"Good. Kitchen was hotter than hell today. I definitely need a cold shower, but I brought you a present." I slipped my backpack off my shoulder and dropped it to the floor behind the couch.

"You don't have to buy me things."

"Then you don't want this lunch I worked so hard on for you?" I pouted as I walked around the island and came to stand close to him.

He playfully glared at me. "It fucking smells good, and I haven't had lunch yet."

"I know, you told me, so Felix let me try out a recipe, and he said he was going to add it to the lunch specials."

"Congratulations." He leaned in to kiss my cheek, and I turned my head slightly so his lips landed on the corner of my mouth. His lips were surprisingly soft, and the tease of his mustache made me need to take it further. Instead, all I did was stroke my hand across his lower back.

In the previous weeks, I'd upped my touches, tried to build a comfort level, and eased him into intimacy. I gave him a second brush to the corner of his mouth and noticed his lids lowered, and he seemed to lean into me. He was almost there with me. Any indecision I may have had about pursuing making my baby mine had ended weeks ago. Yes, I was a cautious person. I had to be in order to keep the life I had, but I was also young and tired of denying myself what I needed.

"First, try this." I handed him the cup as I shoved a straw in the top. He took it, and I focused on him, seeking out even a hint of pleasure. Feeding him made me happy. He took a sip and moaned, and that rumble went straight to my balls.

"What is this?"

"Milkshake made with bourbon-infused vanilla toffee ice cream."

"This is fucking amazing, babe."

"Thanks. I used your favorite brand when I made it this morning." I didn't like when his gaze dropped as if he didn't expect me to do something special for him. Reluctantly, I turned away to open the bag and pull out a clear, plastic to-go box. "Now this, smoked brisket with an espresso rub and a sweet and spicy slaw with french fries."

"Did you bake the bread, too?"

"Just eat it, smart ass." I rubbed his furry belly and walked behind him to get a bottle of water from the fridge. The gruff *damn* made me smile as I glanced over my shoulder to see him go in for a second bite. He chewed slowly with his eyes closed.

"Do you need a new job?" He placed the sandwich back in the container and spread his hands on the counter. I couldn't help studying the dark blond hair on the backs and wondered how those strong fingers would feel digging into my skin as he begged me to fuck him.

"I kinda like the one I have, but would there be any perks since I'm friends with the boss?" I asked and then took a big swallow of the cold water and set it on the counter.

"What perks would you want?" he asked, and I couldn't help but smirk.

"Let me think about it while I take a shower. You finish your lunch. I don't like when you're hungry." I removed my t-shirt on my way to pick up my bag where I'd left it. Turning my head, I glanced at him to find him fisting his hands on the counter, and I hated the internal battle he was fighting to pretend he didn't want me.

Was it so foreign the way I treated him that he didn't know how to process how I felt about him? That night we were going on our first date, but to be honest, we'd been dating for months, but he just didn't realize. "Baby, did I leave my green dress shirt here?"

"Yeah, I had it dry-cleaned and hung it in my closet." He distractedly answered.

"Thanks." I walked toward the steps that led to his loft and jogged up them. I'd just stripped down to my boxer briefs when I felt I wasn't alone.

"Dallas, can I ask you something." His voice slightly broke and I spun, throwing my clothes toward his hamper near the closet.

"You can ask me anything. You okay?" He kept his gaze locked on the floor, and his hands were clenched at his sides.

Fuck it. We'd waited long enough. My feet sunk into the area rug as I crossed the floor. I sighed at finally feeling his big, furry body against mine, and wrapped my arms around his waist. I leaned in and only had to tip my chin a bit to push my lips to his. The firm curves conformed to my fuller lips, and I nipped at the bottom one, sucking at it.

"Dallas, what are you doing?" He never paused in kissing me even as he asked, the question muffled against my mouth.

"I think I'm kissing you. Do you want me to stop, baby?" I met his gaze as I gently pressed my mouth to one corner and then the other of his. "You gotta tell me what you want. I think I've made it clear recently what I need. My patience is gone, Lee." I sunk my fingertips into his lower back as his arms came around me, his biceps resting on my shoulders. "Fuck, baby." I slanted my mouth across his and used my weight to move him until I could slam him against the nearest wall.

A deep rumble vibrated his chest where his hairy one met the smooth plane of mine. I teased the seam of his mouth with my tongue until he opened for me. Our breathing was harsh, and he tried to hug me tighter as if I were going to leave him. He'd done the same every time we'd fallen asleep together.

As his tongue teased mine, I touched him wherever I could reach. And as I pushed the cotton of his sweats over his hips, he froze. He tore his mouth from mine and tipped his head back, even better. I sucked at the exposed length of his neck, traced it with my tongue, and moved lower. My cock was ready for whatever as I palmed his fuzzy ass cheeks. An eternity seemed to have passed waiting for him to give in—to let me love on him. The curls on his chest tickled my nose, and just as I was about to see if my baby's nipples were as sensitive under the stroke of my tongue as when I scraped them with my nails, he stiffened.

"Dallas, Dallas, wait...wait a minute."

"What, baby? I was working my way to the good part." I brought my left hand up to fist in his silky hair and tugged hard, and he arched his back. I'd never wanted anyone as much as him. I was barely holding on to my control. I'd dreamed of us too long in his big bed, him naked beneath me as his strong thighs gripped my hips. My dick was so hard it fucking hurt.

"Dallas, please, give...fuck, you gotta..." He was stuttering, and even as he was trying to tell me to slow down, he was rubbing his cock against my bare stomach. Pre-cum spreading across my skin. I watched the desire and indecision make his features harsher.

"Easy, baby, just relax." I placed tender kisses all over his face, he was still thrusting against my stomach, and I memorized every moan and hitch in his breathing. "It's okay. Look at me, please."

He seemed to be trying to take deep, calming breaths. I loved how intensely I turned him on but on the other hand, I didn't like the emotional pain I saw in his pretty, blue eyes.

"Deep, even breaths," I whispered as I grabbed his pants where they were bunched at the top of his thighs and pulled them up. "Come with me." It killed me to separate from him, but at that moment, he needed something else from me. I laced our fingers and started backing up, bringing him with me until I could get us stretched out on the bed. The way he tightened his hands on mine as I'd tried to release him broke my heart. He was so terrified of giving into me, and I didn't understand what I'd done to make him react that way.

We laid on our sides, facing each other. I shifted until I could bend my arm and rest my head on my palm. "Talk to me, and then we'll lie here, take a bit of nap to decompress, and then I get to take you on our first date."

He looked at me, and the shock was clear. I smiled at him as I stroked his side with the backs of my curled fingers. To physically connect with him eased all my worry about if I'd worked enough hours, would my savings account hold up under my tuition payments. The stress of having enough time for him while I tried to balance work and school with my compulsion to be with him. With him, it all just faded away, and that's why I couldn't give him up.

"But to be honest, I've been dating you for months. I was waiting for you to notice. I know shit's complicated because of Carolyn and Taylor, and you might not want them to find out. That's fine...for now. School starts soon, and we might not get to see each other as often. But I want this. Baby, say something."

"You're serious?"

"Very. Is that okay? Do you need space? I can do that. I won't fucking like it. You have a lot better options than a perpetually stressed college student. I mean, you're sexy as fuck. Who wouldn't be tempted?" I asked as I bumped his nose with mine and felt better when I caught his small smile that quirked up one side of his mustache. "Lee, I just want a fucking chance. I haven't even looked at anyone else since I met you."

"Bullshit," he whispered his denial.

"Not bullshit. I didn't understand what it was, but once I did...don't get me wrong, it wasn't easy. You're the first man I've ever been attracted to, but that in no way changes what I want with you."

"I almost left the lake house. You were in the fucking room next to mine. I wanted you naked. I wanted to suck you off. I want..."

"There is one thing. It needs to be said before we agree to anything. I won't share." My tone hardened at even the implication of another man touching him. "While we date and see where this is going, and if we do this, there won't be a time when an open relationship will work for me. If that's something you need, we can walk away right now and stay friends. All we've done is share a few kisses. But I know I can't love on you and walk away."

His left hand stroked across my cheek, his fingers curved around the back of my head, and jerked me forward. The big man whined as our mouths met, and I pushed forward until I could roll him to his back. I lifted until I could shift my lower body to rest between his spread thighs. When I braced my forearms on either side of his head, he smoothed his hands down my back. I rolled my hips as his fingers pushed under the waistband of my underwear.

"You really think this old man is sexy?"

My only answer was to rub my hard length against his, and I smirked as his thighs shook where they gripped my hips.

"Every hairy inch of you has played a part in my jack-off sessions for months. Why do you think your shirt is always hiked up in the back when you wake up, or my arm is down the front of your t-shirt? So, we doing this?"

"Yes."

"Exclusive?" I held my breath waiting for his answer, hoping it was the one I wanted to hear.

"I already told you I'd tried to close my marriage with

Roger, but I realized I didn't give enough of a shit to fight him on it. I can't imagine sharing you."

The subtle roughness of his fingertips stroking up and down my back felt so good. I'd been waiting fucking months to be right there. To not have to pretend that I didn't want to touch him—love on him.

"I even tried to call some of my former hookups, but I couldn't...I wanted you too much."

"Then you know what we're going to do?" He shook his head and then lifted to stroke his lips over my smooth chest. "I'm going to take you on dates, and you're going to let me. And when I think you're ready, I'm going to fuck that tight ass until you're begging me to goddamn stop." The corner of my mouth lifted as his hips jerked. "Because I may be awkward and don't know what I'm doing half the time, but when I get you, I'm going to take you when and how I want, and you're going to offer me that hairy ass like a slut. Understand me?" He hooked his lower legs around the backs of my thighs and nodded. "Good boy."

I slammed my mouth down on his as my left hand went to his thigh and hiked it higher on my side. My baby better be ready for what he agreed to.

14
LEE

We stood in line outside the theater, the movie we wanted to see had an eight PM showing, and we'd barely gotten out of bed in time to get ready. It was all too fucking surreal. He'd broken me earlier. The lunch, the flirty way he'd asked about the perks of working for me, and the touches. When he'd left the kitchen, I'd stood there, hard and needy, still trying to figure out what the fuck I thought I was doing.

I hadn't even been conscious of going in search of him and finding him standing beside my bed in nothing but his underwear. I'd felt like I was about to hyperventilate at what I was about to do, and he'd taken it all out of my hands. When he'd kissed and touched me, my brain went into fight or flight, and he'd eased back. I'd never had a panic attack in my life and hoped to never have one again.

When lips brushed my shoulder through my white dress shirt, I turned to find him smiling at me. His gaze dropped to my mouth, and I willed myself not to get turned on as his hand slipped beneath the back of my shirt. He teased the patch of hair at the small of my back.

"You still okay with waiting until the movie is over to get dinner?"

"Yeah, I'm good."

"I'll get you some snacks when we get inside."

"You're obsessed with feeding me."

"No, I'm obsessed with making you happy, and one of the ways I show I care is I provide food." He shifted to press to my side and twined his arms around my waist, and I lifted my left arm to hold him close.

Public displays of affection weren't something I did in my past. Most of the time, no one even knew I was on a date because me and the person I was with kept a physical and emotional distance unless it was the lead-up to a hard fuck and an easy goodbye. Dallas didn't allow either of those. I was also trying to make up for the fight we'd had before we left home over me saying I was paying. I knew he saved every dime he made, budgeting to cover his tuition payments. It wasn't like I couldn't afford to cover our dates, but I backed off the minute I saw I'd hurt his pride.

"I'm sorry again about the fight."

"I know you have the money, and dating me isn't going to be a lot of going out on my dime, but when I can, I want to pay. I've been thinking about this date for months."

"Months?"

"Pretty much since I helped you shop."

"Why didn't you say something?" I asked as he released me as the line started moving.

"The fact I believed I was straight but fascinated by you. But"—he pressed his lips to my ear—"a straight man doesn't think about fucking his very sexy friend."

I shivered and felt my face heat. "I did the first night I met you."

"My door wasn't locked."

I chuckled as we reached the ticket booth, and he got two tickets for a psychological horror that we'd both been talking about seeing once it was released for streaming. I'd thought about taking him but felt awkward about asking Dallas out on what I'd consider a date.

He took my hand as we entered the lobby. He ordered popcorn and candy and two drinks. He only separated from me for the span of time it took us to find the theater and I picked seats in the back row on the side. I hated when people sat behind me. We got settled and waited as the seats started to fill, but no one sat near us. As the lights lowered, he tucked the popcorn container in the empty seat and put the drinks in the holders of his armrest and the empty one.

I tensed as he stretched his arm across my legs, curling his hand around the opposite side. His left arm came across his chest and cupped my cheek to turn my face toward him.

"I didn't know how you felt about public kisses," he whispered right before his mouth slanted across mine, and I curved my right hand around the side of his neck.

His pulse jumped beneath my palm as I opened for him, felt more than heard his groan as he pulled my mouth harder against his. While he kissed me, he dug his strong fingers into my thigh. He slowly broke the contact of our lips but kept pressing softer and softer kisses to my mouth until he rested his forehead on mine.

He nudged my cheek with his nose until I turned, then he sucked at the side of my neck, sharply nipping just behind my ear. "I'm never going to get tired of this."

I sunk my teeth into my lower lip to bite back a hitch in my breathing as he kept licking and sucking at my skin. Goddamn, I loved that he was all-in, no hesitation, but it was also overwhelming. I went from barely any affection from the man I'd married to one who seemed to want nothing but to love on me.

"We'll continue that when we get home. Just be a good boy until then." Even his whisper held a dangerous rasp, and I had no idea how he expected me to make it through a two-hour movie and dinner. "I'm gonna suck you so good. I've been dying to find out what you taste like."

I let out a loud groan and was thankful the volume of the movie blocked it for everyone but us. And the cruel bastard turned away as if he hadn't almost made me nut in my jeans with just telling me he was going to blow me when we got home.

"You're awful comfortable about sucking a man off," I whispered in his ear and noticed his smirk in the lights from the screen.

"You're not just any man. You're mine. Just wait until I eat that pretty ass, too."

"Bastard," I hissed, and then he gave me a quick kiss.

Between teasing touches, snacks, and him checking to make sure I was comfortable, we watched the movie. I realized I was enjoying all that stuff. Even Taria and I hadn't dated. We went places and hung out as a couple, but we went from friends to a couple without much mentioned.

The movie was good—a few scares and an ending that wasn't too predictable. Maybe worth a rewatch on our couch later. The lights came up, but he remained seated until everyone had left. Then he stood, threw our trash away, and held out his hand for me to take. I didn't even hesitate to lace our fingers.

"Before we go to dinner, want to see where I work?"

"Sure. Do they know you're showing up with a boyfriend?"

"They've all been giving me shit about being all secretive and not letting them meet my man. So I don't think anyone's going to care."

As he said that, something popped into my head. "Do you want to tell Taylor and Carolyn?"

"Yes, but that decision has to be up to you. I've told Carolyn for months that I met someone I really liked. It's been killing me not to tell her it was you, but you have to be okay with it. Baby, I can wait." He softly smiled at me, and I knew he was telling the truth.

"When I told you Taylor was over, that didn't mean I didn't want you there."

"I know, it bothered me, but I also understood it. When it's right, I'll make them both their favorite foods as bribes."

I couldn't believe how much lighter I fucking felt. There was no stress weighing me down. No intrusive thoughts that the younger man was out of my league. Whatever happened, I wanted what we had to work out. I'd questioned myself for months since I'd lusted after him at the lake, but he wanted me. We'd be good.

"Are we dressed good enough to go in?"

"We're just going to head toward the back and hit the bar on the way out. Then there's this Thai place I've been wanting to try, and I know it's one of your favorites. I'm going to have to look up some recipes for you."

Sometimes I wondered if I'd get used to how he seemed to go out of his way to do special shit. Dinners he researched to make because I mentioned they were my favorite. The contentment I felt when he walked through the door after work or him being there when I got home. To look back on the previous months, he hadn't been wrong. We'd kind of been dating, and I hadn't noticed. I opened the door, and a hostess headed toward us with a professional smile until she spotted Dallas.

"You finally design us worthy of his presence?" she said jokingly. "I'm Lila, and you're the mystery man who has our Dallas all smiley."

"I'm Lee. Nice to meet you, Lila."

"I'm taking him to the back, but we're not staying. I planned dinner elsewhere but wanted everyone to meet him." Dallas said, and we spoke to Lila for a few more minutes, and he took my hand and led me through the place. This was high-end. I'd had meals at establishments like that, but they weren't places I felt comfortable frequenting.

"Folks, we have a twenty top coming in," Dallas announced and was greeted with curses and banging pots until they realized he wasn't working.

"You're an asshole, honey," a gorgeous man with sweaty, curly black hair grumbled.

"Yeah, yeah. Felix, this is Lee. Lee, this is the chef."

I noticed I was under intense scrutiny and started shifting a bit uncomfortably at the stares and the once-overs as if they were judging if I was worthy. Then as if on cue, everyone smiled brightly and introduced themselves, and there seemed to be a theme about how happy Dallas had looked lately.

The last person I met was his boss, Edwin, but it was a quick introduction as he and his wife had a sick grandbaby at home, and he needed to get meds. He did tell me that I'd have to come with Dallas on one of their Mondays when they had a huge employee dinner. They tried to do it once a month.

When we were back outside and headed to get dinner, he wrapped his arm around my waist. "Not too painful, huh?"

"I can't believe you told them about me."

"Why? I spend a majority of my time with them. For the most part, we know everything about each other. Partners are our favorite gossip, and I liked bragging about the great guy I liked. I just needed to make sure he liked me back."

We got to the restaurant, were shown to a table, and spent a few hours leisurely having dinner and talking until it was closing time. We'd talked about what would happen when he went back to school and how much he was looking forward to getting it over with. He asked was I still happy with my decision to buy into the pub and how I was doing with the employees. We discussed childhoods and parents, and it seemed no subject was off-limits.

And as it got later, I grew impatient to get home and have him to myself. As much as I wanted the blowjob he promised, I just wanted to go back to my apartment to have him all to myself. He'd made the place a home for me. Those were dangerous thoughts so early, but I couldn't deny what I wanted.

Instead of walking when we finished eating, he ordered a car to take us home, and I was relaxed. He never stopped touching me, and unlike in the past, I didn't want him to stop because it was him. He only let me go long enough to take care of tipping the driver, and we got out in front of my building. In silence, we made our way up to my floor.

"Baby?" I turned before unlocking the door to find him watching me. "Do you want the evening to end now?"

"No, but I have to explain some shit when we get inside." At telling him I wanted him to come in, he nodded.

I typed in the code and pushed the door open, then I hit the switch that turned on the lights on either side of the TV mounted above the fireplace. My eyes closed as Dallas pressed flush to my back and pressed a kiss to the nape of my neck as he gripped my hips.

"Baby, I love being able to touch you." I arched my back, pushing my ass against this groin, and felt the thick length of his cock notched between my cheeks. "Now, what do you need to tell me?"

"This isn't about fucking for me. Yet as much as I've fucked in the past, I kinda feel a little out of my element here." I let him spin me to face him.

"Explain."

"I've never needed some emotional connection with some-one. Sex is sex..."

"Since this means something to you, you're freaking out on me." He smirked at me, and I glared at him.

"You don't have to be amused."

"I'm not, baby. I'm feeling special and smug...happy. Let's go to bed and see what happens." He lifted his chin and brushed our mouths together repeatedly as he moved me back-wards towards the stairs. Then he took my hand and led me up them.

Why the fuck did I feel so goddamned nervous? I didn't have an answer other than this would change everything between us. When my big hands cupped his cheeks as we stepped off the top step, the small amount of ginger scruff teased my palms. "Fuck, Dallas, you're so beautiful."

As he started working on the buttons of my shirt, I was too distracted by the full, soft curves of his lips. My body went on autopilot as he stripped off my shirt and dropped it to the floor behind me.

"No, baby, you're the beautiful one," he rumbled as he started where he'd left off in the theater, his lips and teeth teasing my neck, but he didn't stop there.

I fisted my hands in his hair as he nuzzled the thick fur that started at my collarbones. The feel of his thumbs teasing my small, pebbled nipples preoccupied me until the backs of my legs hit the bed. My throat tightened as I tried to calm down and rein in this uncommon neediness.

"Hey, you pulled away from me," he whispered as he leaned back to see my face. "What went on in your head?"

"I feel needy."

"I hope so, none of that macho bullshit when I'm about to love on you. Be as needy as you want. What we do together isn't wrong."

As he spoke, he dropped to his knees, removed my boots and socks, and undid my belt. I held my breath as he popped the button on my jeans and eased the zipper down. I stared at his face. Would he change his mind? I was terrified he'd tell me we were a mistake.

A groan rumbled up deep from his chest as he stripped my jeans off until I was naked in front of him. He licked his lips as he stared at the hard length of my cock. He grabbed my hips and my shaking hands flew to the back of his head as he buried his face in my pubes and inhaled, and then I felt the brush of a kiss.

"Get on the bed, baby, and lie down on your back, spread your thighs for me." I'd never heard that amount of gruffness to his smooth baritone before, and my cock and balls ached too fucking much to disobey the obvious order. "Where's your supplies?"

I motioned to the nightstand where my lube was and realized I didn't have condoms. "Shit, all I have is lube." I hadn't needed the damn things in over a year. Being with Dallas was just a dream, so I hadn't bothered to stock up.

"It's fine. Now do as I said."

I turned, bent over to crawl onto the bed, and flipped to lie on my back. I slowly lifted my legs and let my knees fall to the side. When I got enough courage to look at him to see what he thought, his pupils were blown and his chest moved with his harsher breaths.

I was about to say something teasing until he quickly exposed every inch of his lean, muscular form. The hair on his legs was light, his bush was neatly trimmed, and his cock, while shorter than mine, was thicker. My hips shifted, thinking about him fucking me with that pretty dick.

He finally stretched out beside me, and he lifted my left leg to rest over his. "I've never seen a sexier sight than you spread out...ready for me." He didn't give me a chance to answer.

I whined, fucking whined when he took my mouth in a brutal kiss, and his right hand slipped between my thighs. I squeezed my eyes closed as he teased the hair around my asshole. The pleasure had my breath hitching as he massaged my hole and taint with firm yet teasing strokes.

"I think my baby likes that." I almost protested as his touch disappeared until I heard the quiet snick of the lube top, and then cool, slick fingers were back.

"No one has ever fucked me before. I've always topped." I stuttered out as he teasingly pushed in just the tip of his finger. My body tightened at the pressure, but I refused to close my eyes. I needed to see his expression the entire time.

"Would you prefer to fuck me?"

I sharply shook my head. "Maybe one day, but I've been dying for you to fuck me. God, I've been thinking about it. My toys aren't enough." I could feel my heart beating out of my chest and sweat started to mist my frame as he shallowly fucked my ass just with the tips of two fingers.

"That's because it wasn't my dick you were riding. I think I promised you something earlier."

I opened my eyes, confused at what he promised. Then the realization hit me as he knelt between my thighs and my arms flew up, and my hands gripped the headboard as he sucked my balls, rolled his tongue around the heavy sac. Then he was loving on every inch of my groin and inner thighs but avoided my dick.

"Suck it," I ordered.

"I don't think you understand you're not the one in control here." The sting of his hand on my inner thigh and then the other shocked me as he surged up to sit back on his heels. He grabbed the towel he'd left on the bed earlier and cleaned the lube from his fingers. "When you're in our bed, Daddy is the one who says when you get that dick sucked or that ass eaten. I say when you've earned my dick. Turn over and present me what's mine."

Something like fear filled my gut, but it wasn't a physical fear. No, it was an emotional terror that he had every weapon to completely destroy me. I shook as I turned over. A bit of shame overcame me as I kept my cheek on the mattress and reached back to spread my crease open to show him what was his.

"That's exactly what I wanted to see, baby. You're such a good boy. No one knows how to treat you as good as I can."

A shiver worked up my spine as his strong hands stroked from my ass cheeks, over my back, and curled over my shoulders. I clenched my hands around my ass cheeks as he pressed his hips to my ass, his hard cock pushed into my crease, and he blanketed my back. His hands braced his weight on either side of my head.

"I love all of this." He stroked his cheek over the hair on my upper back, and the feel of his balls rubbing against my hole made me let out another one of those submissive whines. "It's the first thing I noticed, and I was obsessed with finding out if all this fur was coarse or soft." I held my breath as I rutted my ass, riding his dick with my crease, and I groaned as he took my cock in his left hand and stroked in a slow, almost too soft rhythm. "Baby, you're not going to come. That's for me when I suck you off."

The second he stopped talking, he met each lift of my hips with a grind of his own. Every move was as if we'd done this a hundred, a thousand times as he loved on me. Time ceased to exist. This wasn't what I was used to, some prep, grab a condom, and fuck until orgasms were achieved. This wasn't fucking.

I was so close, but I fought it as I released my ass cheeks, found his right hand with mine to lace our fingers, and my left went to his hair. He was so smooth and lean, physically perfect, and I grunted with each jacking motion of his fist.

"Daddy is gonna breed this pretty ass one day."

"Da—Daddy, I'm..." I stuttered as I tried to tell him I wasn't going to last, and I shouted as he made a ring of his fingers at the base of my cock. I shoved my face into the thick comforter. All movement ceased as he kept the pressure in place until I got control of myself, but I still felt too on edge.

"I said no." He released my dick and straightened. His hands gripped my hips, and I nearly begged him to just get it over with and fuck me, but in shock, he flipped me to my back.

My eyes flew open as his shoulders pushed to the backs of my thighs, and he swallowed my oversensitive cock and sucked me like a fucking pro. He relaxed his jaw and opened his throat when I bottomed out and swallowed me all the way down. Making suckling and snuffling noises as he buried his nose in my thick bush. I squeezed my thighs around his head, and my upper body bowed off the bed to watch him as he gave me head with a look of pure bliss on his face.

Every muscle in my body felt as if they were on fire, and the way I struggled to breathe terrified me. The louder my whines and moans that I'd found embarrassing earlier became, the more he groaned and sucked harder. I panicked as I tapped his arm to let him know I was about to shoot, but he just sucked me all the way in, and my release hit me. I couldn't breathe as intense pleasure stole every bit of sense and reality until I collapsed.

"Fuck, baby." His voice was harsh as he laid on top of me and his lips touched mine, his tongue thrust inside to share my cum that still coated his mouth. The head of his cock pressed to my hole as he jacked off, and my heels sank into his ass. I scratched his back with my short nails. His right arm hugged my head as he tucked his face against my neck, arching his hips, and wet heat spread over my hole, taint, and cheeks. He shifted his hips until his cock notched along mine and kept thrusting. His release-covered hand curled under my right thigh.

I was amazed at the intensity of his release and the way it made me feel. That all of it was for me and I laid there dazed as I closed my eyes and hugged his sweaty body to mine.

"Sorry."

"Sorry?" My heart broke a bit at that single whispered word. Did the regret hit him already? I'd thought I'd have at least until the light of day.

"I'll do better next time."

"Better? What the fuck do you mean better?"

"That was just a quickie. You deserved better for our first time."

I pinched him because I didn't know if he was serious or not. "That was quick for you?"

"Yeah, not my best work." He sounded so regretful as he gently kissed my lips as I knew I was still looking at him like he'd lost his mind. "I'll make it up to you after I get some rest. Let's go get in the shower and clean up. While I love our couch, I've been looking forward to sharing a bed with you without you trying to hide with clothes."

"I needed the protection so I didn't do something stupid." I lifted my head to brush my lips to his. "Not that it did much good."

"I'm putting condoms on the shopping list on the fridge, but when you're ready, we can go get tested."

"I've always used a condom before."

"Me too. But one day, I want to fill that tight ass." My cock jerked, and he smirked. "My baby likes that idea. Let's get cleaned up before we make a mess."

I reluctantly let him go and watched him get off the bed, he stood beside it, and I couldn't stop looking at him. That man craved me, and I couldn't wait to see where we went.

"Come on, love, you're going to get uncomfortable."

I nodded because there was a mess between my legs, and I turned over, knee-walked off the bed, and groaned as he wrapped himself around me from behind.

"Thank you," he whispered against the side of my neck.

"What?"

"For trusting me. You're gorgeous and perfect to me, and I want to keep you so badly."

I didn't know what to say, and I think he sensed it because he grabbed my hand and led me to the bathroom. He turned on the shower and gave me a soft smile as he pulled me inside with him. As he washed every inch of me with loving touches, I thought about how much I wanted him to keep me, too.

15

DALLAS

My phone ringing made me groan as I tightened my arm around Lee, who was cuddled up with his back to my side. I reached out and grabbed my phone. I checked the display and frowned as soon as I saw Mom and Dad on the screen. What the fuck? It was too early in the fucking morning for the bullshit I knew was coming, but she wouldn't stop until I answered.

I connected the call and pressed the phone to my ear. "Yeah."

"Dallas, can you show some manners?" I rolled my eyes at my mother's voice. It wasn't as if she hadn't considered me a burden since I wouldn't do what my father asked. She probably wished my father had worn a condom the night they mistakenly made the disappointment.

"A second in, and I'm already a disappointment. Is there a reason for this call at"—I looked at the alarm clock—"eight AM?"

"You didn't come home for the summer."

I pushed a frustrated breath through my clenched teeth. The same bullshit, just a different goddamned day. "Mom, I told you when I talked to you that I would be working through the summer to save up for my tuition, just like the summer before and the one before that." Lee groaned as he shifted and turned over. I lifted my head as I brushed a kiss to Lee's mouth, and he sleepily smiled at me.

"We requested for you to be home for all holidays. A good son—" I knew what was coming.

"I know I am not the good, obedient, God-fearing son you put in the request for with the big guy. I don't need to keep being reminded of that." I'd long gotten over it, it used to hurt, but in the last four years, it was more annoying than anything. "I'm not coming back. If you were so concerned, you and Father would actually come here, but you're not. I'm just not falling in line." I rubbed Lee's back as he hugged me tight. "Even when school's over, I'm not moving home. When is that going to sink in?"

I smiled as Lee kissed my stomach and then crawled over me to get out of bed, and I didn't take my attention from his nude form until he disappeared into the bathroom. My mother calling my name made me realize she'd been talking, and I'd paid no attention.

"I was distracted and didn't catch any of that. I just woke up."

"Why are you still in bed?"

"I had a date, and we didn't get home until late."

"Christian girl?" she asked.

Lee came back into the bedroom and stretched his arms over his head, and I couldn't contain my groan. "No, I don't know my boyfriend's religious affiliation or if he even has one." The silence on the other end of the connection lengthened, but I heard the freak-out building. I knew my mother and father too well.

They could have their meltdown. The only thing that

mattered was the sweet, burly man making his way back to the bed. "He's coming back to bed. Maybe we can skip the next phone call. I think it would be best for me and your family."

Lee still looked sleepy, and I spread my legs to make room for him to lie down on his belly, and use my stomach as a pillow. She still hadn't spoken, so I disconnected the call, tossing my phone to the other side of the bed. My fingers combed through his soft, sleep-mussed hair.

"Good call from home?"

"Nope, but they never are. Three years and Mother still calls to guilt me for not coming home for holidays and breaks."

"Maybe they could change," he said.

"It's not outside the realm of possibility, but in this case, no. My parents always treated me as the spare son...the unwanted one. There wasn't a time growing up where I felt like a part of the family. When I was about fifteen, I stopped all pretense of caring. It's a five-hour drive to get to me. It's not like I live in another country or even thousands of miles away, five hours, and not once have they come to visit. It's been months since she called me last. I think it was Christmas. She actually skipped Easter."

"I'm sorry." He lifted his head to rest his chin on my stomach, and I stroked his cheek.

"No need to be. I think after you've learned your place in a family that's supposed to love you unconditionally but doesn't, you disassociate from the family structure. Carolyn and her family were more than enough. I spent most of my time with them. Enough about my family. How are you?"

"I'm good, but we have to get ready for work soon."

"I know. I wish I didn't have to go."

"I have to work, too, and I've known your schedule for months. Being night people works in our favor and..." He paused and lifted, crawling up until he straddled my hips. I curved my hands on his outer thighs. "We just have to make it a year. I don't have any issue with your schedule with work and school."

The way he was saying we just had to make it a year meant he wasn't dismissing we had a future. A very long one, I hoped. "Fuck, I love you from this angle, and I don't have enough time to take advantage." The previous night, I'd lost my head, feeling that big body beneath mine, and I'd barely hung on.

"Daddy." His guttural voice calling me Daddy firmed my dick in an instant. "You're going to fuck my face before we get ready for work."

I smirked as he uncovered me, and I barely prepared myself before he sucked the fat head between his lips and took me all the way to the back of his throat. Damn, my baby was born to suck my cock. He gave a nasty one, too, suckling loudly as spit coated my dick. I curled my hands in this hair, and he opened wide as I forced him down until his throat flexed around the head.

I jerked him off me. "Hands and knees," I ordered as I moved to kneel on the bed, gripped the base and placed the tip to his lips, and thrust. I arched as he gagged in surprise as I fucked his face. Snapped my hips and slowly withdrew, repeating as he whimpered and hummed.

"Fuck, you're a good boy for Daddy." My face heated and sweat beaded at my hairline, drops tickling down the indent of my spine. "So pretty." I dragged my short nails down his back, combing through the curls of his body hair. Loving everything about him as I doubled my pace as my balls tightened, and I forced my eyes to stay open.

His eyes were closed, and a flush highlighted his cheeks as he worked for his reward. He was so fucking perfect, and I wasn't going to ever let him go. The depth of my feelings should terrify me, but I craved him too much.

I groaned as I hugged his head to my groin and shot my load deep in his throat as he swallowed every drop. And I watched him as he sucked my cock clean as my arms fell to my sides. I curled my hand under his chin and lifted him until I could get to his mouth. I wrapped my hand around his cock. The other one pushed between his cheeks to play with his needy hole.

He fucked my fist as he thrust his tongue into my mouth and I tasted myself, and I shook as I remembered the way his flavor had filled my mouth the night before. His hands shot up to grip my face as he stopped breathing and dropped his forehead to mine as he arched and came hard on my abs. I stroked him until he whimpered for me to stop.

"Goddamn, Dallas, I..." His voice broke.

"It's okay, baby, just breathe." I stroked his hair as I gently brushed kisses over his face. "I adore you, you know that, right?" He nodded, and I smiled at the big man acting shy. "I have to get showered and home to get my uniform for work. I'm scheduled for brunch service."

He tightly gripped my waist to keep me in place. "Are you coming back tonight?"

"Do you want me to come back?" He nodded, and something felt off. "Baby, what's wrong?"

"It's...nothing, I just need time to fucking process, Dallas, in my forties or not, all of this is weird, but a good weird. I'm...I'm scared of how attached I am to you already."

"You're not the only one, and I have no intention of letting you get away."

"You go shower while I clean up in the guest bathroom and get the coffee started for us."

"I definitely need it." I pushed my mouth to his and then got off the bed, and I glanced over my shoulder to find him watching me. The desire and possessiveness in his gaze made me feel good, especially since it's something I'd never wanted until him.

I had to focus on getting ready, or I was going to be late. I was going to have to order a car to make it home and drive my car to work. Maybe I'll bring some of my uniforms there so I wouldn't have to rush away. I wanted to spend every second with him that I could. With this being unusual for both of us, we had some processing to do, more him than me. I may be young, but I was all-in, and my gut told me Lee was the only one I'd ever need.

16

LEE

Tom and his husband, Loren, were being annoying as fuck. Loren had been staring at Dallas for almost thirty minutes. But I couldn't blame them. I mean, my man was gorgeous. I'd mistakenly told Tom that Dallas was coming to have a pint with me after he finished with his early shift and he'd instantly called Loren to show up. He was taking it all in stride, though, content to sit there having his drink with his left hand curled high on my inner thigh.

"Is he real? He can't be real. No one is this pretty in real life... he's a walking goddamned filter." Loren sighed heavily, and Dallas snorted as he lifted his pint to take a swallow.

"It's a good thing I'm not the jealous sort," I grumped as I stroked Dallas back.

"Baby, you know everyone else besides you is second best." He winked at me.

We hadn't had a repeat of our sleepover after our first date. My night shifts hadn't aligned with his days. I also had a feeling he was trying not to overwhelm me with too much too soon with more than a few blowjobs. Although, I was having a hard time sleeping without him. After two nights in the same bed and the times we shared the couch, I'd quickly become used to him being there. He was also trying not to pressure me to tell Taylor.

"How long have you two been dating now?" Tom asked.

"Officially, a week, unofficially four months."

"Unofficially?" Loren smiled his thanks at his husband as the man refilled his drink.

"He didn't notice we were dating." Dallas rolled his eyes, and I groaned.

"I was clueless, but someone wasn't exactly forthcoming with their bi status."

"That's because the bi status wasn't there until I met you."

I clenched my teeth as he looked at me all innocently as he stroked the backs of his fingers over the front of my jeans. Before we crossed the line into a relationship, I'd thought I was his sole focus, but the way he was before had nothing on how he catered to me since it became official. He called or texted to make sure I'd eaten and how I'd slept if he didn't spend the night. He'd kiss and touch me for no reason. It was affection without the expectation of getting something from me.

"How did you meet anyway? Tom wasn't sure, and I need all the info."

"Spring break, my friends thought they were being sneaky about shit and suggested a week at the lake. I'm constantly working to cover my tuition, so between work and school, I was burned out with not a lot of wiggle room in the budget to take spring break. Lee didn't know Taylor had set it up. I walked in, and a naked man was wondering who the hell I was."

"Must have worked. It got your attention." Loren looked all bratty.

"I didn't exactly know what it was until we ran into each other a few weeks later in the city. A week after that, I took him up on his invite for a friendly drink. I figured he'd fight me about my age, the *straight* thing, and being friends with Taylor, so I slowly romanced him until his guard was down."

Loren placed his chin in his cupped palms and sighed. "The confidence of youth, I so miss my *no fucks given* attitude."

"Babe, you told the police commissioner last week he was a liar at a press conference. You definitely give no fucks." Even with the frown, you couldn't miss the pride in Tom's voice over his husband. Loren was an investigative journalist who really didn't have a sense of personal safety, but he'd gotten better over the years. Tom's blood pressure thanked him.

I sat back and watched my friends playfully argue, which I'd learned was their form of foreplay, and occasionally turned my focus to Dallas to take in the way he seemed so comfortable there. My friends loved him, hell, I was more than sure that I loved him, but I couldn't shake off my brain telling me to be cautious.

The old-fashioned bell above the door drew my attention to see who was coming in, and I groaned as Roger appeared. The disgusted look on his face told me I was in for some bullshit. I hadn't seen him since we signed the papers, and I could've kept on going without him making an appearance. He was dressed in a perfectly tailored suit, not a hair out of place, and after we'd separated, I'd started to wonder what the man saw in me. The sex was great, but other than that, I'd realized we'd had nothing in common.

"Baby, you okay?" Dallas asked as he squeezed my leg to get my attention, and I inclined my chin to the man making his way to the end of the bar.

"My class of clientele just went down," Tom muttered, and Loren giggled at his husband's irritation.

Dallas leaned to the side. "Roger?" he asked, and I just nodded in answer, and I took in Dallas's profile as he studied my ex-husband. He shrugged his shoulders, and as he finished off his pint, he ordered another.

Tom seemed happy for the distraction and headed farther down behind the bar. Roger sidled up to me, and I didn't miss that he noticed Dallas's hand on my thigh or the fact he was rubbing soothing circles on the denim.

"Lee."

"Roger, what brings you in?"

"I heard this rumor you bought into this...place. Thought you'd handle your investments better and the company you keep."

"Pretentious prick," Loren muttered, and Dallas chuckled.

"I made a solid investment, and I'm quite happy with the company," I said as Dallas winked at me.

"You better be," he growled as he leaned to the side and stole a kiss before he straightened and then thanked Tom for the refill.

"Can I speak with you in private, Lee?" Roger's voice was extra crisp, and if I wasn't mistaken, he'd fisted his hands in his pockets.

"Dallas, you okay with that?"

"Go on, I trust you, but don't be too long. I want to get you home. I still have to make you dinner."

"Finish your drink, and I'll be right back." I hated when he took his hand from my leg, and I stood. "We can talk outside." I didn't want to be alone with Roger. His surprise appearance made me suspicious. Even when we'd met in his lawyer's office, he'd barely greeted me.

Roger didn't say a word as he returned to the exit, and I followed behind him. Once outside, I stood in front of the large window that had me in full view of Dallas. He may be calm and said it was okay, but I also didn't want to give him any reason not to trust me.

"What do you want?"

"I need you to come back."

I frowned at him. "No." A harsh laugh slipped free. "In what world did you think I would return after you and Brand pushed me out of the club we worked our asses off to turn around?"

"What? Is this place better?" He motioned to the front of the building with a sweep of his arm. "You're not making a third of what you were at the club. Some dive pub near the college, what the fuck were you thinking?"

"I was thinking I was buying into a business that has almost seventeen years of steady growth. A relaxed, laidback neighborhood pub that also brings in the college crowd when school is in session. So, cut the shit, what did you do? You want me to buy back in? Did your new partner fuck you over somehow?" As soon as I asked, his face turned harsh, rage turning his skin red. "Ah, that's what this is all about? The piece of ass did something."

"He ran after he cleared out all the business accounts."

I applauded karma but refrained from showing my amusement. Brand had only been our partner in the business for a year before the affair was discovered. His money was good, and everything cleared, but I never fully trusted him. But Roger swore we needed an injection of cash to update the club to attract higher-end customers. We'd done just fine for years without changing our formula. Clubs and bars were a dime a dozen most of the time. One would pop up, do well, and then fold for no reason other than poor management or the lack of proper promotion and branding.

"And what does that have to do with me?"

"You're going to buy back in. I had to transfer all my funds to pay this last month of bills, inventory, and employee wages."

I looked at him shocked. During the financial disclosure of our split of assets, he'd had enough money to keep his extravagant lifestyle for the rest of his life and still have money left over. Covering everything for one month wouldn't have stressed him at all.

"What the fuck have you been doing with your money, Roger? I know in detail how much it costs to maintain the club on a monthly basis. Even if Brand cleared out the business accounts, you had more than enough to personally float the club until you could turn things around."

"Business has dropped off in the past year. Improvements didn't pan out."

"I still don't understand what that has to do with me. We're divorced. I have no stake in the club. You made it quite clear you wanted to cut all fucking ties with me to go on with your life with Brand. I'm not coming back, and I'm not bailing you out. I put everything into that place for a decade, and I'm gone for a year, and you've run it into the ground. That's your mistake to live with. Now, handle your own shit. Don't come around here with your bullshit again." I was angry that he'd fucked up everything we'd built. Put our employees in the lurch over thinking with his dick.

"That's unacceptable. We were in this together for fifteen years. You can't even help me out with this?" He wasn't yelling, but that was only because appearances were too important to him.

"No, I can't. I have my own shit to deal with. A son to get through college. A business to run that I enjoy. Making my boyfriend happy."

"That little barely legal gold-digger?"

I stepped forward and pushed into his personal space, lowering my voice. "You can say what you want about me. Be offended that my low-class ass is not caving, but Dallas is off-limits. Twenty-two or not, he's twice the man you are and a way better head on his shoulders. You know what I'm capable of, Roger. I can destroy your fucking ass without breaking a goddamn sweat." I could get him black-balled with every supplier we had. He'd burned so many bridges with his attitude towards those he believed below him that, with a few phone calls, I could make it where he couldn't even get a cleaning crew in at night. "Do you understand me?"

I finally saw the fear in his eyes, and he backed up. My fists were clenched at my sides, and rage still tightened my chest.

"Baby, come inside." Dallas's voice held an edge of command, and I glanced at him to see him standing in the entrance with the door held open. "We have plans."

"Don't come back here, Roger," I warned and stormed around him. The second I got within arms' reach of Dallas, he twined his arm around my waist.

"You okay?" he whispered, and I nodded.

"Yeah, I'll explain when we get home." He tipped his chin up, and I dropped a kiss on his lush lips.

I glanced back to Roger to find him glaring at us. I knew that look. His pride was wounded by being told no and that someone else had control over me. Dallas tugged me inside, and the door closed. He tucked his hand under the back of my t-shirt and stroked my lower back. His touch and presence calmed me down, but I also knew this wasn't over. Roger didn't take kindly to being defied. He just didn't get how hard I would fight to protect what was mine.

17
DALLAS

S oft snores came from the bed. I leaned in the doorway and took in my baby curled up in the middle of what I'd started to consider our bed. He had a pillow hugged to his chest. He'd been pissed off when we'd arrived home the previous night after his argument with Roger. We'd shared a shower, then I'd given him a massage until he'd fallen asleep, and I'd held him until I'd drifted off.

I'd never met Roger, but after seeing him, I couldn't imagine him with Lee. As I'd observed them through the front window, I'd never seen my baby that tense. They hadn't seemed to fit to me. Arrogance rolled off Roger in waves, and Lee was laidback, preferred to be home or at the pub having a pint. I'd had a moment of comparing myself to the man Lee had spent fifteen years with.

Insecurity over being a college student, someone who worked to make sure I could afford to live and pay for my school, and I didn't think I showed my baby enough attention. Yet I couldn't let him go, my decision hadn't changed, and I was sure I was the best man for Lee. I could make him happy, and he'd never doubt he was loved.

I left him to sleep and went to the kitchen to find something to make for breakfast. Lee's sweatpants hung precariously on my hip as I scratched my chest and stared into the fridge. I needed to do a grocery order because Lee always let things get too low. I'd taken over the shopping, and it worked better because I was the only one who cooked in this relationship. He tried to cook for me, even fought me when I said I'd do it, but I had an innate compulsion to take care of all his needs.

Closing the fridge door, I stretched across the island to grab Lee's laptop and opened it to log into his account. As I started to add things to the cart, my baby's steps told me he was coming down. I didn't straighten, just stayed there, leaning over the counter. He looked so cute and sleepy when he appeared, his gorgeous body completely bare, and without saying a word, he circled the counter to lean over my back, hugging my waist as he rested his cheek on my shoulder blade and his facial hair tickled my skin.

"Morning, baby." I lifted my left arm to reach back to rub his head as I continued shopping and let Lee slowly wake up. I groaned as his hard cock rubbed against my ass. My pants had dipped enough to expose my crack, and he rutted against me as he sucked at my shoulder.

I stretched my arms back to grab his hips as I rolled my hips, and he let out those needy, little whimpers that were only for me. He felt no shame in how we loved on each other, and I was dying to fuck him, but I was happy with the blowjobs and hand jobs, or any way we could get off was fine with me.

"Baby, you want Daddy to play with you before breakfast?" His shy nod rubbed his cheek against my back, and I pushed up and turned in his arms. I spun him until we worked together to get his fuzzy ass on the counter and parted his thighs with my narrow hips. "My favorite way to wake up is with you." I gently kissed him as he stared at me from beneath his heavy lids. I groaned as I spread my hands over his lower back and savored the perfection of the strong muscles and the hair under my palms. "You feel so good." I jerked him closer so I could feel every inch of his chest and stomach against mine. I shivered as all that perfect fur rubbed my smooth skin.

"You think so, Daddy?" He shyly kissed me, and I adored how vulnerable he allowed himself to be with me.

I let my gaze move down his chest, the curve of his belly, and to his dick. I loved to feel him on my tongue—pushing into my throat. "Oh, yeah. Do you like how Daddy makes you feel?" I asked as I circled the base of his cock with my left hand and slowly jacked him, keeping the pressure light to tease him.

He called my name, his shuddered moan past his lax lips as he hugged my shoulders and pressed his forehead to mine.

"You're not answering me, love."

"Shit, I love when you call me that," he confessed as I lovingly brushed my lips to each corner of his mouth. He whimpered as I avoided giving him a proper kiss. "I want you to fuck me, please." He begged in that gruff voice of his, and I started to kiss my way down the front of his throat, over his chest, buried my face in the curls, and inhaled his natural scent and the subtle lingering trace of his soap I'd used to wash him before bed.

I licked over the curve of his belly, and just as I was about to get that perfect dick in my mouth, his hands tangled in my hair. I realized we weren't alone as two gasps made him and I tense.

"What the fuck?" Two voices yelled, and I groaned as I jerked my baby off the counter to hide his nakedness with the island.

"Shit," we groaned in unison, and I was still hidden behind his bulk.

"Dallas?" Carolyn whispered my name.

"Can I get him dressed before you yell at me? Wait right

here, baby," I told him as I held up my sweats and jogged up to get him a pair of pants and returned, dropped to my knees to dress him.

I glanced up at his face and saw he was scared. I tried to smile reassuringly, but I knew he was prepared for them to tear into us. As I got to my feet, I pulled the pants up his legs. "Baby, no matter what, I adore you."

"Me, too," he whispered, and at the same time, we took a deep calming breath, and he turned to face Taylor and Carolyn across the expanse of the counter.

"What the hell is going on here, Dad?" Taylor asked as he slowly set a bakery box down and reached for Carolyn's hand.

She still hadn't looked at me since I came back into the kitchen to dress Lee. I rubbed my baby's lower back in support as I knew he tried to figure out what to say—how to explain everything. We'd kept our secret for almost five months and weren't clueless enough that the omission may not be met with much happiness or congratulations. Yet I wanted it to be okay for Lee.

"I ran into Dallas one night after he got off work. We started spending time together...I fought it, honey, I did, but I fell for him and..." His voice broke. He loved his son more than anything, and it was killing him that he wasn't going to make Taylor understand.

"Is this where you've been staying?" Carolyn asked.

I turned my head to smile at my baby and leaned my head forward to brush a kiss to his bare shoulder. "Yes, we started hanging out, coffee, calls, and texts, movie nights here after I get off work, sometimes a pint or two. We didn't go on our first date until recently. I was waiting for him to notice how I felt."

"But why didn't you tell us? You're both adults. Why the fuck keep it a secret?" I couldn't decipher exactly what Taylor's tone was.

Lee cleared his throat before he answered. "He's your friend, Carolyn's best friend, and the more time we spent together, I liked having him just to myself. I'd wanted him since the lake house, but I fucking kept it to myself. I just couldn't resist spending time with him. We've been working shit out, deciding what this is."

"What this is, baby, is I'm keeping you." My voice hardened at his *working shit out* excuse. This wasn't working shit out. He was mine. I'd struggled too hard to claim him.

"Is that true, Dad?"

He nodded. "Yes, sorry, Dallas. I'm..." I crossed my right arm over my chest and cupped his cheek to bring his mouth to mine. All the tension instantly dissolved, and I smiled against his lips.

"It's okay, love. We're not exactly at our best. I didn't get to make them their favorites. We're bribe-less." I felt better when he softly chuckled at me. "I love you, okay?" I ignored the choking from the other two people in the room with us. Lee's eyes widened, and that shyness was back—that was all my baby.

"I love you, too," he whispered.

My attention came back to my friends. "I love him. You can be pissed about us keeping it secret, but it was best for us. This wasn't easy. My only priority in this world is to make Lee happy and feel loved. You may yell now, but I need to feed my baby soon."

Taylor and Carolyn stared, their gazes bouncing from me to Lee and back again as I tried to figure out what they were thinking.

"You owe me fifty," Taylor yelled at Carolyn.

"I thought you were joking when you said you saw his name in your dad's phone. You cheated," Carolyn accused.

"What the fuck is going on?" Lee asked me as we watched them argue over the specifics of a bet. He wrapped his arm around my waist, and I twisted to hug him and place a kiss to his chest.

"You're not subtle, Dad, and sunglasses work but not when you're directly staring at the object of your obsession. Also, when you didn't come home that night, Dallas, there was obviously a man who groaned the next morning when you called her." Taylor grinned. "We already figured out you were spending the night with a man or someone non-binary because you started to default to we or gender-neutral pronouns when talking about this person. When you always used female pronouns before."

"We weren't expecting this, though. At least I wasn't. Taylor cheated with inside info."

"How did he have inside info?" Lee asked Taylor.

"I clicked on your text messages when you weren't looking and saw Dallas was the last one. Would you have ever told us?"

"Son, I was working through this attraction I had to a much younger man who happened to be friends with my son. A gorgeous man I assumed was straight. So I fought it so it wouldn't ruin your friendship or put stress on your relationship with Carolyn. And I didn't want to give up what I had with Dallas even if all we ever did was hang out as friends."

"Is this an open relationship, like with..."

I instantly cut Taylor off. "Fuck no, it was one of our first agreements. At no time would I be willing to share. Also, I didn't tell him. We've been dating for months. I was just waiting for my baby to figure it out. But our official date wasn't long ago. Not that we're not happy our kids stopped by, but why are you here so early?" I relaxed as my friends snorted.

"We stopped by the bakery and picked up some stuff, figured we'd stop by to see Lee. No reason to take them back to the apartment since you didn't come home." Carolyn's tone was all bratty.

"I'll make coffee. Baby, I started our delivery. Could you add the things from the list? I'll finish it after I figure out what I'm cooking this week." I gave him a quick kiss and flipped off Taylor when he gagged, and then I started to make coffee.

Lee pulled the list from the fridge, and I saw him tense. I'd marked off condoms and a new bottle of lube the day before. They were already stored in the nightstand on my side of the bed. I smirked as he seemed to come back to himself. I glanced over my shoulder to see him and Taylor sit down at the bar with the laptop.

"You could've told me, Dallas. You're my best friend."

I rubbed her back as she seemed a little sad, and I hated that I'd done that. "I know, but I wasn't sure that he was going to give in. He fought it hard. I was preparing to get hurt if he ever put distance between us. It had nothing to do with whether I trusted you or not. It was more I was trying to protect myself from too many questions later if he rejected me."

"You love him, huh?"

"Yeah, have for a while. How couldn't I? I mean, look at him. He's fucking perfect. I'm pissed I didn't get to play with him before the kids interrupted."

"Bleach the fucking counters," she hissed at me, and I snorted.

I hit the brew button and then went to take care of her order before she had a meltdown. While I did that, I glanced at Lee to find him grinning at me. I winked at him and mouthed *later.* I knew we had to make it up to Taylor and Carolyn, but that didn't mean I wasn't impatient to have my baby all to myself. I'd gotten used to not having to share him with anyone, and I'd found I was damn greedy when it came to Lee.

18

LEE

"If I'd known you had kids when we started dating, I would've rethought this relationship," Dallas hissed where he was physically trying to kick Carolyn and Taylor out of the apartment.

I ignored the chaos happening in my normally peaceful home as three grown-ish adults play wrestled at the door. One of them being my boyfriend made me rethink my life choices. I just shook my head as I finished cleaning up the kitchen from dinner. As the door finally slammed, I was putting the last plate away. Strong, lean arms wrapped around me from behind.

"We're going to have to change the door code."

I closed my eyes as he nuzzled the back of my neck and rubbed my belly through my t-shirt. We'd dressed earlier after our talk with Taylor and Carolyn. We'd had breakfast, watched movies, and ordered lunch, and Dallas had made all of us dinner. As much as I wanted to be alone with Dallas, I'd enjoyed the time I spent with my family. The weight of not telling my son and Carolyn about Dallas and I disappeared.

I wouldn't say terror hadn't overtaken me the minute I'd heard my son's voice. He was hurt, I could tell. All I could hope was he understood why I kept my relationship secret. Whatever I was thinking disappeared the second Dallas shoved his hands under my shirt.

Could you become addicted to someone's touch? Hell, could you become addicted to a person was the better question. I'd always thought it was an impossibility. Sexual partners came and went at regular intervals in my life as we grew tired of each other or found a new regular hook-up.

"Did you mean what you said earlier?" The question had played repeatedly in my head throughout the day. Shock had taken over at hearing him say he loved me in front of witnesses. He always told me he adored me, and I knew he cared—that he wanted me, but I'd tried not to think too much about the L-word.

"What did I tell you the first morning we woke up together?" he asked in my ear.

"Um, that you'd never say something to me you didn't mean."

"Exactly, baby..." He urged me to turn around with gentle pressure on my side. "I know I'm young, but I'm not stupid...I know what I feel. For months, all I could think was I couldn't imagine being anywhere but here with you. I understand your ex did you wrong, and no matter what you say, there's probably some lingering issues. We can work through those. I love you. Did you mean it when you said it?"

"Yeah, it's not something I just pop off with, but..." I sighed and didn't know what I wanted to say or even how to explain. "I had one kinda agreement. I haven't done monogamous since Taria."

"And I told you that's not an agreement I can deal with. Someone else touching you...just the thought pisses me off. If you don't think you can do the one-on-one with me, I'd prefer to know now, and we can just go..." I cut him off by grabbing his face in my hands.

"I don't want you to go. I'm just saying all this shit is weird, not a bad weird. I had a man who supposedly loved me enough to marry me, but that was only if we kept up the same open arrangement. It worked until it didn't." He was so gorgeous and opposite of me. I still didn't understand how I got that lucky.

"What are you thinking about?" he asked as he drew circles on my lower back, and I grinned because I knew what he was doing. He had a sensory turn-on about every hair on my body. Dallas couldn't resist.

"How I got lucky."

He hummed and tilted his head. "I'd think that was the other way around. I'm glad I let my friends force me into going away for spring break."

"We probably would've met eventually. I think my son is in love with your best friend."

"There's no question he is. He's kinda worried about having two more years of school, more if he gets into medical school and her magazine job becomes full-time after graduation. He met some of the guys that work there. While Carolyn's worried because he has years of school left around all those pretty students."

As I combed my fingers through his ginger hair, he tipped his head back, and I dropped a kiss on his full lips. I'd never really seen the big deal about kissing. To me, it had always been about the main event. I did it because my partners liked it, but not something I went out of my way to do. With him, I took every opportunity to snatch a minute of being connected. Non-sexual affection in a relationship was weird for me.

"They'll work it out." I draped my arms over his shoulders and pressed my chest to his. "I love you."

"I know. You want to relax with a movie to decompress since we had to entertain for a majority of the day or..." He smirked as he tucked his fingers in the back of my jeans and slid lower until he could squeeze my fuzzy ass cheeks. "We could go back to bed and finish what we started when we were so rudely interrupted."

"Bed, but I want to get ready first." He pouted, but I brushed my mouth to his and clenched my back teeth as his fingertips stroked over my hole.

"I'll make sure everything is locked up and turn down the bed. Take your time." I saw the reluctance in his expression as he released me, but I needed a few minutes.

I slipped around him and hurried up to the loft. I wasn't scared of bottoming. Hell, I used my toys enough that I knew I loved it, but this was different. When I entered my bathroom, I closed and locked the door. I needed to take a shower and prep. The vulnerability was back. As a top, I was confident and always made it good for my partners—no one had ever complained.

As I got ready, I focused on the motions and tried not to get lost in my head. Yet that wasn't really working for me. I was this strange mix of scared and excited, throwing in a little good old-fashioned insecurity. Which was stupid. Dallas had his face buried between my cheeks plenty of times. He'd seen every inch of me, and I was sure he was a little more than obsessed with my body. I was feeling awkward and fucking psyching myself out like I hadn't had sex more times than I could fucking remember.

I'd taken longer in the shower than planned and rushed to get out, and I dried off. Wrapping one towel around my hips, I rubbed my hair with another as I entered the bedroom. As soon as the door opened, one corner of my mouth twitched as I watched Dallas throw the covers to the foot of the bed.

I couldn't help taking in every inch of pale, smooth skin, the way his lean muscles moved beneath it. He lifted his head and smiled as he caught me. His gaze stroked from my head to my toes, and I groaned as he stroked his cock as he looked at me.

"Come on, baby, time for bed." He held out his hand. I hung my one towel on the door handle and padded across the room.

As soon as I laced my fingers with his, he grabbed my other hand and twisted my arms behind me. He trapped them at my lower back as he buried his face against my throat. He placed open-mouthed kisses across my collarbones, and I dropped my head backward as he sucked one nipple and then the other.

"If you're nervous about me fucking you, I'll bottom."

"No, I've been dying for you to fuck me."

"No is a complete sentence. If at any point it doesn't feel good, we stop. I want you to feel good, and for me, anything we do feels amazing. So fucking sexy."

I groaned as he pinched my pebbled nipple between his teeth, and I arched at the slight pain. I'd never known how fucking sensitive they were until him, but maybe it was just him. Everything with Dallas felt right. As if I'd been waiting for that moment.

He released my hands. "Stay right there." He moved away and turned to slide the drawer open. The new bottle of lube and a few condoms landed on the mattress where he threw them.

I didn't take my focus from him for a second as he crawled onto the bed, positioned himself in the middle of the mattress, and crossed his legs. He patted his inner thighs. My hands shook as I removed the towel and let it fall to the area rug. I lifted one knee and then the other to the mattress, and felt the firm surface give under my weight as I slowly made my way toward him. I straddled him, lowered my ass into the cradle made with his legs, and twined mine around him.

"I've been thinking about this all day. Did you know what I had planned for our day off?" I shook my head. "I was going to suck you off, my favorite way to start my day."

As he spoke, telling me everything he'd planned, my cock pulsed where it was pressed against his flat stomach. He drew his fingertips too lightly up and down my back, I bowed my back to urge him to increase the pressure, but he continued with that teasing touch down my triceps, over my elbows. Dallas curled his left hand around my wrist and lifted it to his lips, brushing a kiss to my pulse.

I almost ordered him to get on with it, we both wanted to fuck, but his expression was so loving. No one had ever looked at me as if I were their center—their everything. When I was with him, I knew no one else existed beyond me and taking care of my needs. After months of selfishness and not sharing him, I'd gotten spoiled. Was it strange that at my age I'd learned how much I loved being owned?

"Do you know how much I love your body?" He smoothed his cheek over the hair on my forearm. "So perfect."

"I think you have a hair fetish."

"Maybe I just have a fetish for you." He repeated the caresses to my other arm. "I love all this hair against my smoother skin. Every time I jerked off before we got together, the contrast made me fucking harder." He leaned his head forward to nuzzle the center of my chest. He let out a moan as he rubbed his face over my pecs. "Doesn't hurt you obey like such a good boy for Daddy."

If I was supposed to say anything, I was shit out of luck when he started loving on me with his mouth, teeth...his hands. Pulling at my hips to rub against him and I hugged his head. I placed the sole of my feet together and shifted my legs wider. For a man like me, feeling as if I was being cherished was odd. I was a big, burly man, hyper-masculine, and no one had ever treated me as if I'd break. Everything Dallas did to me was intoxicating.

There was no hurry. No demands for me to turn over so he

could get off. He savored every second. And all I could do was submit, ignore the ache in my balls and the painful hardening of my dick. Every time I gasped or made a noise of any kind, he'd repeat the caress, the bite, or strong suck, just to hear it again.

My body was restless as our skin grew damp with sweat, and then I hissed through my clenched teeth as cool, slicked fingertips drew through my hairy crack and pressed to my asshole.

"Let's see how much I need to stretch you so you're ready," he whispered against my lips as the tips of two fingers popped past my rim, and I hugged him tighter as I arched my hips backward. "Shit, you get so needy when I play with you."

My thighs shook as he eased in to the next knuckles, retreated, and thrust deeper. As if from a distance, I heard myself begging, and he praised me. Every time I whined or whimpered, he kissed me. Our breathing rushing noisily against each other's cheeks as he kissed me roughly and fucked my ass in slow strokes.

"You want Daddy to fuck this tight, slutty hole, don't you, baby?"

I think I stuttered out a yes, but I wasn't sure. I was too focused on the burn and pressure. When I used my toys, it hadn't come close to the pleasure I got when he finger fucked me. It was as if he knew I needed the pressure—the fullness, and he slipped a single finger deep as he sucked my dick. This, no, this was so much more intense, and I wanted more.

"Turn over and straddle my thighs. Daddy wants to eat that pretty ass before I fuck it."

I probably looked like a fool with how quickly I obeyed, but I didn't care. I was on my hands and knees, my ass in his face as I lowered my upper body. A heavy sigh shuddered out, almost too loudly in the quiet room as he palmed my cheeks. I yelped as he spanked one ass cheek and then the other, I felt his breath on my crease, ruffling the hair, and he continued to smack my ass.

The pain turned to pleasure, and I started to meet every smack of his palms. I pushed back, and then it was fucking heaven. His face was buried between my cheeks as he pulled them wide. He rimmed me. Before him, no one had done that, and I may be slightly obsessed with my Daddy eating my ass. My hands fisted in the sheets as his tongue pressed at the tight muscle, and I lost control. My hips rolled as he increased the pressure until the tip slipped inside.

My heart was pounding, and I could hear it in the rush of blood in my ears. My cheeks flushed, and I felt pressure in my face as I realized I'd stopped breathing and was bearing down. Minutes or hours could've passed. I was so fucking close that my cock was dripping pre-cum. He had an infuriating habit of ignoring my cock until he thought I was ready, but I knew if I tried to stroke myself, he'd smack my hand away. He always told me that was only for Daddy to play with.

Just as I was about to open my mouth to plead with him to fuck me, he gave my hole one last kiss.

"Come up here, baby."

My limbs were shaking as I struggled to turn around. He was breathing heavy, his chest moving with the strain and the head of his cock was flushed an angry red. His pupils were blown as he stared at me. The sight of what I did to him shocked me no matter how many times I saw it—it probably always would.

I flipped to my back and laid down, my thighs wide as I stroked my right hand over my cock, and groaned at the desire that was almost pain. "Daddy, please."

"I'm going to take such good care of you." His baritone once again filled with that dangerous rumble as he got to his knees.

He opened one of the condoms with shaking hands and almost froze, smoothing the latex over his dick. His throat worked as he swallowed hard and closed his eyes, seemingly to calm himself down.

Too slowly, he moved between my thighs, coated the condom with extra lube, and I held my breath as he braced himself on his right hand beside me. His eyes met mine as I felt the fat head of his cock push to my hole, and his hips flexed. He nudged me several times, and when he breached me, we groaned in unison. My stomach sucked in, there was the burning pressure I expected, but the pleasure was almost too intense as he smoothly thrust until his hips met my ass.

"Ah, shit, baby, you're strangling Daddy's cock." He gave me a few shallow pumps, and my breath hitched as I placed my hands under my knees and pulled them up and to the sides. He shifted a bit as he lay on top of me. The tip of his nose touched mine and braced his forehead on mine as he started to move.

My cock was trapped and rubbed between our bellies as he worked his thick length in and out, slowly at first, steadily building in rhythm until his lean body was rocking us on the bed. Embarrassingly high-pitched grunts slipped out every time his hips slapped against my ass. I grabbed his ass, feeling the flexing of muscles with every pump. I kept reminding myself to breathe, to relax, but it was as if my body was no longer mine. It belonged to only him as he used me in the best ways possible.

The easy glide out. The brutal slam forward. I hitched my legs higher to lift my ass off the bed, and then the real fucking started. He reamed my ass without mercy as I scratched at his ass cheeks, up his back, and the harder I dug, the more brutality he displayed.

"You feel so good, Lee. So mine," he rasped out between brushes of our lips or tangle of our tongues.

"Dallas." I hissed as he hit my gland, and I felt the position of his hips change, and then he was pounding that one spot until sweat and tears wet my face. His hands roughly gripped my hair. Our bodies were shaking under the strain of chasing our releases.

He shot upward, bracing his hands beside my hips. "Jack that pretty fucking cock, I need you to come on Daddy's dick. Baby, let me see."

I almost told him I couldn't as I wrapped my hand around the base and hissed as it bordered on pain. I desperately searched for the lube and added some to my cock as I jerked off to the almost feral rhythm he set until I was groaning as I reached down with my left hand. My middle and index fingers framed Dallas's cock, and I jerked my gaze up to his face, his lids heavy as he stared down at where we were joined.

"You gotta shoot, baby, I'm not—" I saw the way his jaw clenched as I squeezed my fingers on either side of his pumping dick.

I jerked my cock faster, paying attention to the tip, letting it pop through the circle of my fingers. I threw back my head, the tendons in my neck straining as I held my breath and spilled my load over my belly. His pace faltered, and then he slammed in one last time, trapping my hand between us, and he came with a groan that was my name as he fell forward, his head resting on my upper chest as he shallowly fucked me through his orgasm.

I was mentally, emotionally, and physically wrecked as I lay there trying to calm myself. His hands pushed under me and palmed my cheeks as he gently kissed my chest.

"Fuck, I love you," he said with a guttural rasp as he lifted his head and stretched up to meet my lips. "You okay?"

I nodded. "Yeah. Don't you dare say you can do better because I won't survive. I'm not twenty-two anymore." We chuckled as we lay there in a sweaty heap. "I love you, too, Dallas. I really do."

"I know, baby. I gotta get rid of the condom. You want a rag, or you want to clean up yourself."

"Just bring me a rag. I don't think my legs are working right now." As if on cue, my thighs shook where I eased the hold I had on his sides.

"Just relax. I'll be right back."

I held the base of the condom as he pulled out, and he eased off the bed. His legs didn't seem to be holding up any better than mine. I never looked away from the flexing of his ass as he crossed the room and disappeared into the bathroom. I heard the shower turn on, and I dropped my head to the pillow.

I relaxed my legs but didn't bother trying to move. I twisted my head to check the clock to find over an hour had passed. No wonder I was wrecked. Who the fuck had I fallen in love with? I closed my eyes with a sigh and realized I was ready for sleep.

The feel of Dallas washing my hands with a warm rag made me open my eyes. His hair was wavier when wet and fell across his forehead as he stared down at me. His emotions were clearly on display, and I wondered how I'd missed it, or maybe I'd just ignored it, trying to save myself if this ended. He bent at the waist, and I grunted as he sucked my cock into his mouth as he cleaned the lube from my hole and crease with the cooling rag.

I gripped his hair as he rolled his tongue around my soft cock as if trying not to waste a drop of my release I'd spilled. He released me and glanced up at me with a smile.

"I'll be right back. Get comfortable."

I did as he told me, sat up and flinched a little at the twinge of soreness, and grabbed the covers to pull them back up. I curled under them, and then he was back. He wrapped himself around me to hold me close to his chest.

"I'm tired."

"I know, just close your eyes and go to sleep. I want all the time I can get with you before I have to start dealing with work and school again. Shit, baby, I'm gonna miss sleeping in bed with you every night."

I opened my mouth to tell him to just move in, but I bit back the order. But I wanted him there when I got home from work or to get in our bed when he finished work. Dammit, I wanted all the things, but we'd just started officially dating. I didn't want to add any more pressure. We were perfect as is, and one day he'd move in. Until then, we were just right.

19
DALLAS

Fuck school. I cursed internally as I finished with my last lecture of the day, and I was headed straight to work. It was only the first week, and I was already done because I hadn't seen my baby in two days. He was dealing with getting Roger off his ass. His ex-husband had gone radio silent for weeks and was back with his bullshit offer of Lee buying back in.

It was a shitty situation. Lee was worried about the employees he'd left behind and who were probably about to lose their jobs, but on the other side of the situation, he didn't want to deal with Roger. It seemed the man had gone through an obscene amount of money in only a year. Lee had explained that Brand had taken off after clearing out the business accounts but that Roger should've had plenty to float the club.

I had no sympathy for Roger. He'd fucked up his life all around when he cheated on Lee. Yet I also knew that if Roger hadn't, I wouldn't have my baby all to myself. I headed for the parking lot and would call Lee on my way to work. I had no lectures the next day, but I was in the kitchen for the brunch and lunch service. Which meant I wouldn't get to go to Lee's until tomorrow evening.

Digging my keys out of the front pocket of my backpack, I connected the call to Lee with the other hand. With the phone between my shoulder and ear, I unlocked my door and slid in behind the steering wheel as I listened to the rings.

"Hey, Daddy." I grinned as he whispered into the phone.

"Embarrassed for people to find out?" I hit the button to put the windows down. The heat had built up over the day. We weren't due to cool down any time soon.

"You know I ain't. You done with school for the day?" he asked as I put him on speaker and put my phone in the holder to continue talking to him.

"Yes, I'm headed off to work now. I put you on speaker. I wanted to hear your voice. I won't get to see you until tomorrow."

"It's okay, well, not okay, but I get it. Your place is closer to work. You missing me, Daddy?" I heard the smile in his voice. The dirty phone call before bed the previous night so I could listen to him get off wasn't fucking enough. I'd told him so, too.

"You fucking know I do, don't sound all bratty. Your ass is begging for a spanking." I heard a choked cough and turned to find a guy about my age getting into the car beside mine. I winked at the dude, and he rushed to get in his own vehicle. "We shocked a dude next to me."

"I bet that amused you." His gruff chuckle sounded so good.

"It did. How are you doing? Getting things straight with Roger?"

"I demanded to see the financial reports on the club for the last year since I ceased any involvement in everyday operations."

I carefully backed out and then made my way through the

maze of the parking lot until I reached the main road. "Is it bad?"

"It's a cluster of the highest order, Dallas. They began the renovations, but the construction company stopped due to payment issues. The club has two main floors, one of which was for typical customers who just wanted to come in and dance, have some drinks. Second floor was for our more kink-friendly customers. Private rooms. VIP. All those kinda things. They definitely were where the money was made."

"But you told me he was working on upping the class of his customer base."

"Yeah. He was beginning a program for members only that would comprise the second floor. A ridiculous amount of money. I mean, the second floor usually stayed hopping. Our servers and bartenders fought over that assignment. Since he announced a fee, second-floor numbers went down, but also, he started the renovations there. That cut the hours of the employees who were assigned to serve and tend bar there. Loss of income makes for unhappy employees, but the issue is we offered benefits."

Shit, benefits for bar and club employees were almost unheard of, and when they were offered, well, no one wanted to give those up. Especially not to start over at another place. "And since they have benefits, they're less likely to quit."

"Exactly. I called a few of my inside people I still have there. Roger started having private parties of the kink variety after hours. We have some employees who became uncomfortable when asked to serve or bartend. Any sexual activity was for private rooms and were to be marked occupied. Apparently, it's moved out into the open."

"So, what do you want to do?"

I listened to his sigh and wished I was there to take care of him. "I don't know, I don't want to buy back in, but I don't want the people that relied on us to lose everything because Roger suddenly thought it was a good idea to do whatever the fuck he did."

"Drugs?"

"No, I thought of that as an option, but Roger is too careful. Drinks a bit too much on occasion, but most people do that. Rumors are he started plying his hookups with expensive gifts. One was getting rent and bills on a condo paid. He seems to be going through a midlife crisis. Every time he shows up with someone, they're getting younger and younger."

I rolled my eyes as I waited at a red light. "And he called me a gold-digger."

"Don't even compare. What do you think I should do?"

"If you want my opinion, appraise the business as is, there's loss in value, buy the club outright for the amount of debt and a fair amount for Roger to walk away and turn into an employee-owned corporation."

"What?"

"Put control of the club equally in the hands of all the employees. You find one of your employees who has management experience or hire one to do the day-to-day financial operations. All the employees spilt the profits and form a board to vote on any and all changes, like any board of directors." I huffed at the amount of traffic, but also, I wasn't in any hurry to end my call. "You take a larger cut of the profits for a set term to pay back your initial investment and then leave even. You have enough to cover, and you still have fifty percent ownership of the pub so that's income coming in. So you start at an initial loss, but you know the club is profitable with the right management. Go back to what worked and get rid of all the changes that Roger and Brand implemented. As much financial trouble as Roger is in, he'll have no choice. If he turns it down, you can walk away with the clear conscience that you tried."

"I knew I loved you for a reason."

"There better be a lot of reasons, love."

"There are. Namely, a certain part of you."

"Oh, so, my dick was the deciding factor."

"It definitely was." The bastard groaned, and he was getting a spanking the next night.

"There are spankings in your future." I groaned as I pulled around back to the employee parking lot. "Okay, love, I'm at work. Let me know how everything goes."

"I will. I love you, and I can't wait for you to be home."

"Me, too. I don't sleep as well without my furry, weight blanket."

"And I see, I'm just a body."

"A body I adore beyond all reason. I love you. I'll call you tonight when I get home. Have your toys ready."

"Yes, Daddy."

I smirked to myself as I disconnected the call, and as I looked out my window, Edwin was grinning at me. "Hello, boss man."

"Uh-huh, maybe check your surroundings. There's some things I don't need to know about my employees."

I huffed. "You're the one who told me to go with my attraction."

"I did, and happy employees make for a happy boss. Felix is in a mood."

"When isn't he? Chefs have God complexes." I opened my door and rolled up my window as I grabbed my uniform for the bar from my backseat.

"True, how sadly true. Okay, if you have any issues, I'm headed home. Just text me. We have two private parties coming in."

"They're always a pain." I groaned as I got out, locked, and slammed my door. "Have a good night. We probably have everything covered. If anyone threatens to quit, I'll talk them out of it." I crossed the parking lot listening to Edwin cursing behind me.

Most of us threatened to quit at least twice a week, and he was waiting for us to not be joking about it. I entered the back door, said hi to everyone, went to the small locker room to change, and stowed my stuff in one of the lockers. I reminded myself that all I had to do was make it through one more night and shift, and I could see Lee. Only a short time together, but I was already so attached. I had a year left to spread myself too thin, and then I could focus all my attention on my baby. Hopefully, he wouldn't get tired of waiting.

20

LEE

To watch a grown man have a complete tantrum as he looked at the thick packet of papers my lawyer had given him saddened me yet irritated me, too. I'd spent years with Roger, and I wasn't happy about what I'd needed to do. He hadn't given me any other option to take care of the people I felt a responsibility for. A week of discussions with my lawyer and a private meeting with all the employees, I'd come up with a fair offer, just like Dallas had told me. It would work in two parts, save my employees from losing everything and get the club I'd been so proud of back to where it should've stayed.

"This is bullshit, Lee. After all the years we spent together, this is what you think it was worth?" he screamed from the opposite side of the desk and threw the offer on the surface.

"It's a very fair offer. The same amount you and Brand paid me to buy me out of the club and the amount of the mortgage you took against the house to finance the renovations. This place is six months from going under. You can take the offer and walk away or hang out until you leave with nothing. This is the only option you get from me. The minute I walk out of this office, don't contact me again."

"Buy back in and run—"

I was tired of his fucking arguments on repeat of me buying back in. There was no way I was even going to consider partnering with him again. The mess he'd made in less than a damn year was proof he couldn't be trusted. "No, those fifteen years you want to throw in my face ended the minute you lied to me. After going over the accounting and the extreme drop in profits in the past year, my advisor said this is more than generous. Some said I should've offered much less."

"Is this about that little gold-digger of yours? Being led around by your dick."

"Don't be a bitch, Roger. Dallas has nothing to do with this offer." I almost told him the offer was because of Dallas, but Roger was already losing his mind. "This is about my employees that you fucked over. If it wasn't for them, I wouldn't even consider this. But if things don't change, all the employees are ready to walk. You'll be running this place on your own. What's it going to be?" I pushed up from the chair, and my grim-faced lawyer shrugged his shoulder, and then I turned my focus back to Roger.

In a matter of minutes, it looked as if he'd aged a decade. The man I married no longer stood in front of me. I turned my head and asked for a minute with Roger. The man nodded and left, closing the door behind him.

"What the fuck are you doing?" I demanded. "A year ago, I left you with a profitable business. This place could've run for another decade or more, until you were ready to retire."

Roger collapsed in the chair. "You left."

"What did you expect, man? You could've told me flat out that you were fucking Brand, and I wouldn't have batted a fucking eye, but you didn't. You did it behind my back and then demanded a divorce for an exclusive relationship with him. That turns out wasn't exclusive."

He threw his arms out and looked at me with what looked almost like hatred. What the fuck had I done so bad to him? "Why the fuck did it matter who I fucked? It was the same arrangement as always."

"How many didn't you tell me about? That was the number one rule, I didn't have to meet them, but I had to know about them."

"Did you tell me every man you took to your bed?"

I could answer honestly. I'd always followed our agreement because I respected him and his safety, to let him know who I was fucking and check results even though condoms were always used. "Yes, I respected you. You knew of every man I fucked. But how many times did I ask you to end our open relationship? It no longer worked for me."

"What we had worked."

"It worked for you, not me, not the last five years we were together."

"Is it working with that boy?"

"He's my boyfriend. I love him, and he, in no way, wants to share me with anyone else. Before he would agree to be with me, he made it clear it wouldn't be acceptable for him. But he said if it was something I needed, he'd respect that, and we'd go our separate ways. I'm not coming back. If you thought we'd go back to the way things were, not a fucking chance. Take the offer. It's the only one you're getting. Sign the papers, and my accountant will make sure the money is transferred by the end of business today."

I walked over to the door and knocked, and a few seconds later, my lawyer was back. Roger seemed to deflate. All his pride was gone. A business he'd pretty much put everything into for over a decade was on the verge of collapse, and he had no options other than me. I crossed my arms over my chest as he stared down at the papers, and with a shaking hand, he picked up the pen.

Once he signed and initialed everything, he shoved them away and told us to get out. I didn't bother saying a word. Once we were out in the main room, I shook hands with my lawyer, and he left to take care of finalizing everything and call my accountant to authorize the transfer.

All the employees were waiting there, most of them looked stressed, and a few appeared terrified. I'd adored all of them for most of the last several years. I'd built an amazing and loyal team in a business where there was always a lot of turnover.

"We'll schedule a meeting next week to sign the paperwork. If this place thrives or fails, it's all on y'all now. There will be a clause in the contract that my investment will be paid off in no more than two years or at the time of sale. A portion of the profits will pay me off. You'll have to decide amongst yourselves who you trust to take over the financial management or hire someone."

"Lee..." Ariana said as the most senior employee. "...thanks."

"Don't thank me, when we celebrate the transfer of owner-ship, you can thank my boyfriend, it was his idea about the employee-owned company. I hadn't even thought of that until I asked his opinion."

"Still, we appreciate it. You gave most of us a chance, no matter what our pasts were. Leaving here, I don't know if we'd have the same options." Nelson, the head of security, shrugged.

"I'll own the controlling portion of the place until y'all pay me off, but I have the pub and Dallas, and they take priority. Next week we'll discuss everything that needs to happen to get this place back to where it once was."

I got hugs and handshakes, and then I was leaving. Sadness hit me because it was leaving a major part of my life behind. When I'd walked in earlier, I'd had no connection. The pub felt like where I belonged. The only reason I'd returned was to make sure my people continued to thrive. I'd worried he wouldn't take the offer, but as Dallas said, all I could do was offer, and I could say I tried.

"Lee," Roger called my name as I was about to reach my SUV.

I groaned. I was ready to be done and get home, but I pivoted on the toes of my boots. "I think we said everything we needed to."

"But, honey, you know you want to come home. We had a good thing going," He started to touch me, but I grabbed his wrist. I released him, and he dropped his arm back to his side.

"Don't start with your bullshit. At one time, I may have considered it, but the more I thought about it, it wasn't going to happen. What we had ended a long time ago. I have what I want. A job I love. A home to start over in. And as much as you hate it and is probably the reason you're trying to reconcile, I have a man who I love that only wants me."

"He's a kid. He'll grow tired of you...you got some money, and you're giving it to him. Of course he's bending over for you."

"He hasn't asked for a dime, and I'm the one who bends over, and I beg for it every fucking time." His face turned red, and he spun, stomping off to his own vehicle. Okay, low fucking blow, but sometimes that was the only way get the point across.

I got in my vehicle, pulled out my phone, and checked my notifications.

Dallas: *Hey, baby, you on your way home?*

Dallas: *I'm waiting to start dinner.*

Lee: *Yeah, he signed, and I talked to everyone. I'm pulling out now.*

Dallas: *I'll see you soon. Be careful.*

Lee: *I will. Love you.*

Dallas: *Love you too.*

I set my phone in the cupholder, started the engine, and pulled out, heading home. Our evenings were rare since he was going to school during the day and working the evenings. But I knew he was doing what he needed to do. Hopefully, one day, I could talk him into letting me cover his tuition at least. Even if he wouldn't, one more school year, then he was all mine. I could live with that.

21

DALLAS

Rough fingertips stroked along my side, and firm lips sucked at the side of my neck, and I lifted my hand to comb my fingers through Lee's hair. I rubbed my bare ass against my baby's hard dick that was notched between my ass cheeks.

"Morning, baby." My voice gruff from sleep, and I groaned as his left hand moved to wrap around my cock, giving me several strong tugs.

"Can I fuck you, Daddy?" As he asked, he rutted harder against me.

We'd discussed it for months, but every time it came down to sex, he wanted to bottom. Although, I was dying to know what he felt like inside me. In answer, I turned over and slid my leg over his hip, and I pressed my mouth to his as he gripped my ass cheek and moved closer. Almost a year had passed since we met, and I craved him more every day.

"You can have whatever you want. All yours, baby," I whispered as he rolled me using his weight and settled between my legs, and I scratched my nails softly up his back.

Us loving on each other never ceased to shock me in its

intensity. I stretched my arms over my head and gripped the headboard as I arched my back. He tortured me with firm licks over my chest, sucking hard at my nipples, and lower over my abdomen.

He pushed my legs up with his hands under my knees and opened me wider. I glanced down my body to find him lying on his belly. He licked his lips, and I prepared. My breath hitched as he swiped his tongue over my hole. Sucking at the tight muscle, loving on it.

"Shit, baby, I love when you eat my ass."

"Daddy likes that, huh?" he asked but didn't give me a chance to answer because he was too busy pushing harder.

My body twisted as he tongued my asshole, but his hold on my legs didn't allow me to move. I slammed my eyes closed and savored the hot, wet pressure as he worked to loosen me. I'd taken a finger or two during foreplay, but I was beyond ready to know what he felt when I was inside him.

I grunted, bowing my upper body off the bed, and grabbed his hair as his movements became rougher, and I felt the vibration of his groans. I nearly protested when he stopped, but he was stretching to grab the lube from my drawer. He sat back on his heels as he slicked his fingers. He leaned over me, and his lips touched mine, and I whined as he slowly pushed two fingers deep.

"Damn, baby." The burn and pressure, a slight discomfort, but I wanted him so much. I slipped my arms around his neck as he worked to loosen me up. I relaxed as pleasure began to build. I lifted my legs, my inner thighs squeezing high on his sides. I smoothed my hands over his back, feeling a fine sheen of sweat beneath the hair I loved so much.

"Does that feel good, Daddy?" he whispered in my ear.

"Uh-huh, shit, is this what I feel like when I'm inside you."

"Better, I can't believe you're..." His voice broke. "I don't have your stamina."

"I'm sure you're gonna get me right where I need to be." I rode his fingers, getting over the strangeness of it and wanting more. "Fuck me, baby."

"You're not ready."

"I'm ready, do it." He only left me long enough to coat his bare cock and was back. I held my breath as the head pressed to my entrance. He gave a solid yet slow push, and my body opened for him.

We sighed in unison as he bottomed out and he rested his weight on me. He pushed his face against the side of my neck, bracing his weight on his left forearm, and gripped under my thigh as he began to move.

It was right, perfect because it was him, and I held him close as he panted against my skin. I bit at his shoulder as he pumped his hips. My cock getting teased by his belly and the hair that covered it. Almost a year, and I was still obsessed with textures of skin and hair, the way his sweat smelled manly and clean as we fucked.

"Baby, ah, fuck." He hit a certain spot, and I froze. "Right there, love."

The force of his fucking rocked the bed, and I held him tighter as I tried to remind myself to breathe through the extreme pleasure.

"Daddy says his baby has a slutty ass. I think Daddy's the one..." I sucked at his shoulder as he picked up his pace, our sweaty bodies sliding together. His hips slapping against my ass. "You were made for me, Dallas."

He fisted his hand in the top of my hair, and I knew he was close. I'd memorized every sound my baby made when I loved on him. I reached between us, grabbing my cock, and he bowed his back to give me room. I clenched around him and jacked my dick to match Lee's pace.

He turned his head to find my lips as his pace faltered as if he forgot how to move. All I could feel was the perfect glide of his slick cock, the firmness of my grip, and I tried to hold on, but it was too much—too good. I tightened my legs around him, my arm around his neck, and flipped us until he was on his back.

I placed my feet flat on the mattress as I braced my hand on his belly and rode him, bouncing as he cursed under me. He grabbed my hips, and I stared down at him as I worked to get us off. His neck was arched, the muscles straining as he slammed me down on him. He ground his hips against my ass as I felt my sac ache, and my back bowed as I shot all over his hairy stomach. Shaking above him as I did everything to draw out our pleasure, never wanting the feeling to end.

I collapsed forward and sprawled across his chest, both struggling for breath. "You might have to fight me for the bottoming."

He let out a surprised laugh that turned to a groan as his softening cock slipped free. "Not too much. I like bottoming for you, Daddy." He hugged me tight.

"I know. You complain about the extended foreplay, but you like when I make you beg."

"I do. What do we have planned for today?"

"We have to do something after that?" I smiled at his chuckle.

"No, but we have to decide what we're going to do for spring break. Wanna go back to the lake, just the two of us?"

"It'll be like an anniversary," I said as I lifted my head and rested my chin on his chest. "It's where my obsession with you started."

"Really, it was seeing me naked, wasn't it?"

"Oh yeah, I didn't have to use my imagination too much when it came to jerking off."

"Nice, still all about my body. Just a piece of fucking meat. Dallas," he whispered my name.

"Yeah, Lee."

"I want you to move in. I mean, you're already practically living here. What do you actually keep at your apartment?"

"Furniture. You think we're ready for that? You could get sick of me."

"Like that'll ever happen. Seriously though, you're already here most nights. You made this a home, Dallas, and I want you in our home all the time. It'll cut down on the rent and bills you have to pay."

"I can't pay rent here?" I snorted at the dirty look he gave me.

"It's paid for, no rent, and if you want, you can pay half the utilities it if makes you feel better."

"I think I can do that. Our kids have been talking about moving in together. Especially with school ending for Carolyn."

"Then we can tell Carolyn you're moving in here, and Taylor can move in with her."

"Sounds like a plan. Let's get in the shower, we both need one, and then I want a day of lazy on the couch and delivery."

"We can do that."

I dropped a kiss on his smile and then climbed off him, heading for the bathroom, and groaned at the soreness. But it was good. As I entered the room and started to reach in to get the shower going, my baby body wrapped around me from behind, and he spun me to see our reflection in the mirror.

"You're so beautiful, Dallas." His voice was gruff as he stroked my hairless chest and stomach with his slightly rough hands.

"You are, too, baby."

He dropped his gaze, and his shy smile was back. This was all mine. No one else got that side of Lee. The soft, vulnerable man who'd denied a lot of his needs, but with me, he had the freedom to demand them. I took his care and safety, his well-being, seriously. I spoiled him with all the love and attention I had. At almost a year in, I didn't see that changing any time soon. Just as I always knew he was the only person I'd ever need.

EPILOGUE
LEE

My facial hair rasped under my hands as I scrubbed them over my face and stretched my shoulders. Tom had taken off with Loren for a few weeks of vacation, which left me doing all the paperwork we both loathed to do. Luckily, we had great employees who didn't need to be micromanaged. The co-owners of the club had paid off my investment in my former club two years ago, and I often visited with Dallas to see how proud they were of the place they'd built for themselves after they'd taken over. Brand was caught but ended up with nothing but a slap on the wrist when he paid back what he'd stolen. Roger sold everything he owned and took off to parts unknown. He hadn't tried to contact me or Taylor since.

Over the past few days, I'd started looking back over my life. My forty-fifth birthday was right around the corner. I had no regrets about my life. A few things I would've done differently, but not much. As a young gay man, I'd become acquainted with my vices, embraced them, and lived my life to the fullest, or at least I'd tried. Everything I'd done led me to that point, and I had no complaints.

I pushed up from my chair as I made sure everything was turned off and all the paperwork the closing crew needed was where they could find it. I walked around my desk. I turned my attention towards the door as I grabbed my jacket to leave for the day. My heart kicked into a dangerous rhythm as Dallas smirked at me as he closed it and leaned back against the surface. Three years together, two years of those married, and he'd become even more obsessed with me. All my doubts and insecurities had quickly faded at the beginning of our relationship. He was still gorgeous and lean, his hair a bit shaggier than when we met.

"Hey, baby."

"Hey, Daddy." I smiled at him as I draped my jacket back over the chair. His beautiful honey-colored eyes darkened as he crossed the short distance between us.

I moaned as my husband manhandled me onto the edge of my desk. He pushed my thighs open until his chest was flush with mine.

"I missed you," he whispered seconds before his lips met mine, and I opened for him, the tip of his tongue meeting mine. I whimpered as he cupped my ass to pull me closer to the edge.

I broke the kiss with a sigh. "You saw me half an hour ago." He'd taken over as chef and manager of the pub's kitchen, turning the already successful business into a destination for lunch and dinner. We'd even bought the storefront next door to expand into a full dining room. Edwin was still cursing me a year later, but him and his wife were regular visitors.

"Too damn long. You ready to go home?"

"Yeah, I was just coming to get you. Taylor and Carolyn are dropping Paige off in two hours." Taylor and Carolyn hadn't married yet, but they said they didn't need it to be committed, but they'd given us a beautiful granddaughter a year earlier. A bit of a surprise since they'd decided to wait until Taylor finished medical school.

"How long do we get to keep our granddaughter?"

"Just for date night."

He snarled his nose. "We'll tell them to leave her."

I shook my head. "If it was up to you, she'd move in." I wrapped my hands around the back of his leanly muscled thighs just beneath the curves of his ass cheeks. He'd already set up part of the guest room as a nursery and was steadily trying to get Paige to stay more. He was sneakily trying to transfer her to our home.

"Probably, our grandbaby looks just like you. I spoil you both rotten for that reason." I felt his smile against my mouth as he kissed me again, slipping his hands under my t-shirt. "And nothing has changed in almost three years. I still love taking care of your every need. Speaking of need, I'll have just enough time to take care of this." He slipped his left hand between us and cupped my cock through the denim of my jeans. I let out a shuddered breath.

"We have two hours."

"Like I said, just enough time, but I'll make up for the quickie when we go to bed tonight."

All the time together, and he made every time we fucked last until I was begging and screaming for him to just get me off. He'd chuckle darkly and make me suffer longer. He showed me all the time that his need for me hadn't waned. To be honest, he seemed to want me more. All I had to say was Daddy, and his eyes darkened as his pupils dilated and he was dragging me to the nearest available surface.

I wouldn't tell Tom how many times we'd used our shared desk over the years. I raised my hands and pushed his hair back from his forehead, feeling it was slightly damp with sweat from working the kitchen.

I dropped my gaze just the way I knew he liked as I looked up at him from under my lashes. "Do you still love me?"

"More every day, Lee. You're even more beautiful than the first time I saw you." He cupped my face and traced my mustache with his thumbs. "Let's go home and enjoy our night." He kissed me, sucking at my upper lip and then my lower one, crowding my body with his as if he couldn't get close enough.

Everything had led me to him. If I'd had a different life, I don't think I would've appreciated him as much as I did. He pulled me off the desk, picked up my jacket, and I rolled my eyes as he helped me put it on. He laced his fingers with mine and led me from the building. This was as close to perfect as anyone could ever get.

ABOUT THE AUTHOR

Siobhan Smile is an author of happily ever afters with a twist. They features characters of all sizes, shapes, sexualities, gender identities, and races. Reading a Siobhan Smile book lets you escape for a few hours whether that is to an alien world or a contemporary setting, you'll find something outside the norm. Writing books for Siobhan is more than simply telling a story, it's a way for everyone to see themselves get a HEA.

   Author Pronouns: Nonbinary/Gender Nonconforming - They/Them

ALSO BY SIOBHAN SMILE

WRITING AS J.M. DABNEY

Cold Cases Unit

Cold Cases and Second Chances

Cold Cases and Dark Secrets

Cold Cases and Bitter Enemies

Cold Cases and Bruised Hearts

Cold Cases and Zero Witnesses (Coming Soon)

Sappho's Kiss Series

When All Else Fails

More Than What They See

Dysfunction it its Finest Series

Club Revenge

Soul Collector Prophecy

Twirled World Ink Series

Berzerker

Trouble

Scary

Lucky

Brawlers Series

Crave

Psycho

Bull

Hunter

Executioners Series

Ghost

Joker

King

Sin & Saint

Trenton Security

Livingston

Little

Gage

Pure

Masiello Brothers

The Taming of Violet

3 Moments Trilogy

A Matter of Time

The Men of Canter Handyman

Black Leather & Knuckle Tattoos

Chance at the Impossible

Bloody Knuckles Bar & Grill

Clipping the Gargoyle's Wings

Standalone

By Way of Pain (Criminal Delights - Assassins)

Christmas, Bloody Christmas (By Way of Pain Xmas Story)

Waited So Long

An Odd, Little Girl

Claiming Whisper

Adoring Beast

A Yuri Sorenson Mystery

Not Another Statistic

Permanent Freebies

Has the Honeymoon Ended? (Brawlers Short Valentine's Story)

Once Upon a Bear Claw

The Scars She Bears (Executioners Short)